FEET IN THE FIRE

The Redemption of Howard Marsh 3

Bob McGough

Bearded Bard Inkworks

www.beardedbardinkworks.com

This arc of the Jubal County Saga could be called
Found Hope.
So each part is dedicated to a different group who helped
me find my Hope as an author.

To my Siblings,
Mark, Heather, and Anthony.
My childhood wouldn't have been the same without you.
I learned something important from each of you...
...like what my capacity for annoyance was.
Worth it.

Contents

An Introduction to Howard Marsh

Howard Marsh is a lot of things: a liar, a thief, a poor man's wizard. He's a shoddily tattooed skin stretched over a too skinny body that's barely held together by the same drugs that are tearing his life apart. A cynic, his words are often as poison as the substances he takes to pass his days, a suicide attempt years in the making.

He's the scion of a family with a history as rich as it is materially poor. He's the product of a miserable county with more dirt roads than paved, where poverty and loss is the order of the day. He's a man haunted by his past, and has yet to find any reason to try and piece himself back together.

You would be well advised to take what he says with a large grain of salt. He will cover the worst parts, glossing over the bits that show his darkest sides. The bits where the drugs that ravage him are in control. Where we find him is at the bottom, eking out a living as a water witch, a copper thief, a finder of lost things. Living in a storage shed and trying to maintain what's left of his frayed relationships with the few family members who will still talk to him.

But dear readers, he's a better man than he thinks. He doesn't see it; he's long forgotten the possibility even, and no one left in his life sees it either. But, if you can endure the miserable existence of watching someone make nothing but bad choices for a time, then you will perhaps be rewarded. Maybe you will see him slowly scrabble out of the muddy, trash filled ditch that is his life.

It won't be quick, and it won't be painless. The stories to come are often filled with sadness. The fairytale ending is not for stories such as these. There is a chance at happiness, but it is a long way away, and there are many obstacles both in him, and in his path.

This is not a plea for understanding, or forgiveness, or any sort of justification. It is just the way of things.

He is Howard Marsh, the Methgician.

And he doesn't give a damn what you think.

Dusty Roads

Being the Fifth Tale in the Redemption of Howard Marsh.

Stealing My Heart

I froze as a dog began barking.

That started my heart pounding a bit, not going to lie. But it pretty quickly became clear that whatever the damn thing was barking at wasn't me. So I could get back to my thieving.

It's hard work being a degenerate sometimes, I mused, and leaning back, I wiped my brow with my arm. I was pretty sure doing that not only managed to wipe away the sweat but also smeared a good amount of grime and dust across my forehead. I was probably quite a sight, but there wasn't anyone around to see me. Or at least there better not be, else I was gonna be in real trouble.

My heavy gloves wrapped back around the metal plating keeping me from the copper inside the old air conditioner and pulled. I really put my back into it till I heard a pleasing snap. Diamonds may be a woman's best friend, but copper wire was mine. Thankfully, it was the metal giving way and not something in my back. Growing older was hell, I was led to believe, but I was doing what I could to ignore that fact, and so far my body was obliging me.

I didn't exactly plan on living long enough to get old noways.

I'd taken it to mind to actually do something to treat Anna, do a real sort of date for a change. Not sure why that idea came up on me like that; it certainly wasn't my usual style, but damn it, she wasn't my usual type of woman. She had all her teeth, for example. And a job. And no kids! Which, in Jubal County terms, made her just about the most eligible bachelorette around.

But dates cost money, and money was usually best spent on drugs, which I would of course share with her—least ways the ones she was actually willing to take—but that did not a fancy date make, I reckoned. And what few dollars I did have were gonna have to go to my usual upkeep expenses, like Pop-Tarts and meth.

The fates, however, had aligned, and in one of my little walkabouts around Elk Grove I had spotted an unattended house with an equally unattended air conditioner. That got me in mind to actually be a bit more productive than usual. So, I broke out my favorite copper-stealing gloves (that I had actually stolen from the Christian Mission drop-off) and decided to go earn some money the old fashioned way: with my standard dishonest work.

Even being nighttime, and not all that warm, I had worked up a real sweat. But it was all paying off. I had two more houses after this already scoped out, and with copper prices being what they were, I was about to be well on my way to having some date money.

I was humming my copper-stealing song, just really getting into my groove, when I saw the pale gold glow of headlights coming up the road. I ducked down low behind the AC unit, which, big as it was, I could lurk behind unseen easily enough. It was annoying to have to stop, seeing as I was just about to secure the copper coils I was after. But better safe than sorry, I reckoned, so there I hide.

And damn me if those lights didn't slow down and then come to a stop right out in front. They were far enough forward that I could see the nose of some sort of dark-colored SUV, which wasn't good. That usually meant a rich person or a cop—or even worse, some sort of fed. But seeing as copper theft wasn't exactly high up the FBI's list of crimes, that meant it was probably one of the locals.

All that got confirmed when they cut on that spotlight thingy they have attached to the side mirror. It flicked on, and wouldn't you know it, it honed right in on the fucking AC I was hiding behind. Which wouldn't have been a problem five minutes ago, before I had showed up, but right then it was clear as day by all the scattered bits and tools that someone had been trying to liberate some copper. Then I heard the slam of a car door, and I knew it was time for me to make my daring escape.

Years of smoking things that should never be smoked had wrecked my lungs to the point that I couldn't run five steps without wheezing. But, all things considered, I was fast as fuck. Being strung out means you don't carry around a lot of excess weight, let's say.

I made sure I still had my gloves on—those, I didn't want to lose—and then I took off. The grass hadn't been cut in months, but it didn't slow me down any. I ran full tilt for the tree line at the back of the yard like a hellhound was right on my ass. I heard a shout, something probably telling me to stop and throw my hands up or some such shit.

I just threw up my middle finger instead, laughing like a fucking loon for a second, up until my lungs told me to stop that shit. I decided to risk a look back, and sure enough some local cop was chasing after me. But it was clear they didn't stand a chance; I had way too much of a lead on them, especially as I was right up to the tree line.

My head turned back just in time for me to run right smack into a limb.

They say karma's a bitch.

That fucking branch wasn't thick enough to lay me out. It was, however, thick enough to blacken my eye and stagger me. It was only the thought of jail time that kept me moving forward, even if my gazelle-like sprint had turned into something more like a drunken stagger. I could hear that shouting getting closer, and I knew I had to get moving or I was done for.

At least I was in the woods now, which gave me a chance to hide. Staggering forward, I managed to strike up something like a fast jog as I hunted some distance to put between me and Johnny Law. It was sure enough dark in those woods, so I stood a bit of a chance, I thought.

Behind me I could hear the boy in blue start crashing through the brush too. I decided to veer hard left, since things looked darker that way. It made it tricky, trying to carry on through all them trees with only one good eye, but somehow I managed.

There was a big fat magnolia tree in front of me all of a sudden, one of those real old ones that spread out wide as a house, a snarl of limbs and thick green-black leaves. I parted them limbs like Moses and kept going till I hit the trunk. Magnolias are easy climbing when they get that big, so I decided that maybe my salvation lay upward. It damn sure didn't lay there on the ground, what with decades of dead leaves making a layer of what may as well have been noisemakers.

I don't pray, but if I did, I would have given thanks for them gloves. Even half blind, I was able to shimmy up that tree a good fifteen feet up in just a few seconds, the rough texture of my gloves holding me in good stead. I was even able to sort of shift around to more on the far side of the tree, mostly hiding myself. A flashlight would fuck me up, but folks don't look up much, I've found.

Between my lungs screaming and my heart pounding, I could hardly hear shit. But I could see that cop's flashlight click on, and thankfully it looked like he hadn't zigged when I had zagged and was looking in the wrong direction. Unfortunately he wasn't giving up, and as I began to get my breathing a little under control, I could hear the crackle of his radio.

From where I was, it was mostly static and cursing with not much I could make out. I wanted to know a whole host of things, like if he'd identified me or if there was backup coming, but I also didn't really want him to get close enough for me to hear, if that makes sense. I wanted him far away and steadily getting farther.

He'd stopped running and was sort of looking around now. I don't know if he had given up chasing, or if he figured I'd gone to ground. But he was still hunting–that much was clear. I wanted to cuss, but I knew my luck and was certain that he'd hear it no matter how far away he was.

So instead I flipped him off.

I remember when I was real little and had just learned what that meant. My dad had just beat my ass for something, so I was trying to crawl away without crying, 'cause crying just meant I'd just get hurled into another wall or the like. But he turned his head long enough that I flipped him off. I mean I *really* got into it.

It was such an impotent move . . . but damn if it didn't give me the gumption to just keep on. Black Tom still had a habit of coming around just long enough to beat my ass about some bullshit, but no matter how many bones he broke, he never broke my spirit.

I mean, the drugs did that, let's not get it twisted.

But I say all that to just really express how much I love to flip off folks in authority. Don't matter if they know it or not. I know it, and fuck them.

I eventually figured out it was Fuckin' Brian that was out there chasing me. I'm sure he had a last name, but as the biggest dick among a whole host of assholes, most of us just called him Fuckin' Brian. Not to his face—at least not more than once, as a flashlight-induced former concussion of mine will attest.

The fact he couldn't find me was pissing him right the fuck off, and he kept getting louder and louder. He kept making bigger circles, though, and that meant he was gradually working his way closer to me. And judging from how he was swinging that light of his around, he was looking up on occasion, no doubt checking climbable trees.

My heart, which had begun to ease its racing, started to perk right back up and I started thinking about what my moves were. A quick catalog showed there wasn't shit I could do—not without making a huge ruckus that was sure to draw him right on me. Brian was an ass, but he was an in-shape ass, and he had hawked me down a couple times in the past, given enough ground.

I wished I had some magic that would help me. I knew there had to be millions of spells out there that would get me out of this—to cloak me in shadows, or bathe this whole tree in illusion. But no, my present choices were basically to hurl some fire at him or summon an illusion only I could see. And he'd be fucked if I wasn't even all that high, so it wasn't like I had a lot of juice, even if I had been the kind of person to really hurt someone else.

Fuckin' Brian was Fuckin' Brian. But that didn't mean he deserved to be ate up with magical fire. No one deserved that. Not even my daddy, Black Tom.

Well, maybe him.

I was ready to just turn myself over to the "resisting arrest" beating that was about to happen when some angel of a dispatcher came over the radio, informing all parties concerned that there was a bad wreck over on Highway 19, and could Fuckin' Brian stop chasing that teenager long enough to lend a hand?

The blessing of being a short, strung-out dude . . . Brian thought I was just some kid.

I almost laughed as he set off back for his squad car, cussing up a storm every step of the way. But I ain't quite that dumb.

And hell, the night was still young. With all the cops over on 19, the world was my oyster. After all, all this copper wasn't going to steal itself.

Oh, the Possumbilities

It's a sad state of affairs when your girlfriend seems more fond of your pet than you. When your pet happens to be a fat, usually sticky possum, it's even worse. Has a real way of deflating the ego, it does. And when your pet feels the same way about your girlfriend . . . well, it causes you to take a look at your life choices.

Horace, my possum familiar who typically lived around the Dairy Queen dumpster when he wasn't curled up in front of my little space heater, had rolled his fat ass up the moment he heard Anna's car. I hadn't known possum ears were good enough to tell the difference in car engine noises, but if my lady love drove up, you can bet your ass that Horace would crawl out from wherever he was hiding to welcome her. As usual, I got my quick kiss hello, and then she worried over my black eye a bit. She knew better than to ask how I got it, at least, but I could see a bit of worry in her eyes. But the moment sticky-britches waddled up, I was all but forgotten.

"Horace!" she cried, scooping ol' Lard Belly up into her arms. She gave a little grunt as she picked him up—you don't just lift that kind of weight without some sort of exertion—and began to give him kisses. More kisses than she'd given me, I would note. I could feel the happy waves coming off the little bastard.

Having a familiar had its perks. We couldn't talk or anything, but he could usually figure out what I wanted somehow. Magic, I guess. And I was able to store up a good bit of my excess magic in him for a rainy day. Whenever I tucked some away, his scraggly hair would stick up like he'd been electrocuted, which I had to admit was always good for a laugh. And he acted sorta as a guard dog, but better, really, 'cause I was pretty sure he could see spirits and such now. But times like this . . .

Anna's nose curled a bit. "He smells a little like ruined milk. And he's sticky. He needs a bath."

I had given the bastard a full bath not two days earlier. But I think the prick had figured out if he got extra gross on Fridays, Anna would give him another. And while he fought back when I bathed him—an awful lot like a cat would, mind you—when Anna went to clean him up, he was all about it all of a sudden. "I just bathed him

Wednesday," I said, knowing I was wasting my breath. She cut me a look and I just gave in.

Cop in my grill? I'll be a bit of a shit. Rutherford hassling me? Snark city. HD on my case? Just call me Mr. Sarcastic. Even with Anna, a lot of the time, I'd get a bit sassy. But when it came to her and my damn possum, I just had to throw my hands up. Some fights just ain't worth the grief. It would just end with her going home early and Horace sulking all week. I'm not that much of a masochist . . . well, most of the time.

I rolled out the wash pot Anna had bought at the Tractor Supply in Montgomery and took my five-gallon bucket over to the little spigot at the corner of the storage buildings. The water came out in cold spurts, but quickly enough I had the bucket filled. I managed to get it back over to the wash pot without spilling too much on me, thankfully.

Anna already had Horace in the pot, and slowly I poured the water over him, filling up the pot to about the middle of his round belly. She was already scrubbing him down with some Dawn dish soap. She'd decided that was the best thing to use ever since she saw a commercial about using Dawn to get oil spill gunk off a baby duck. Spilled oil and the muck in the bottom of a Dairy Queen dumpster were about the same, really.

Horace looked over at me. He was grinning so broadly I thought his face was going to split wide fuckin' open.

Smug bastard.

Anna was looking at me too, pointedly. "Well?"

I kindly started. "Well what?"

She gave an exasperated huff. "Start the heater up! Don't want this baby getting sick. It's gonna get cold tonight!"

Fuck my life.

A Marsh Awakens

I woke up slowly, fighting to stay asleep. I wasn't entirely sure where I was at first, my last clear memory being drinking a beer inside of a car that was whipping down the highway. I couldn't even remember what day it might be. Rather than open my eyes, as that would mean I had given in to consciousness, I took stock of what I could.

It felt like I was lying on the ratty fold out couch that Anna and I had found on the roadside a couple of months back. It had been a step up from my cot, if for no other reason than my lanky girlfriend's feet didn't hang off the end. A little Lysol, a lotta Febreze, and it had been right as rain.

The couch was laid out, unfolded into its bed form, so it must have been the weekend. During the week I kept it folded up like a couch and just slept on it like that. I'm not fancy. No, if it was unfurled, then Anna would likely be there.

Scrunching one eye open ever so slightly, I confirmed my suspicions. I was in my storage unit home, and curled up under a mountain of blankets was Anna. She was so bundled up I could barely tell she was in there. Only the top of her head was sticking out, a bit of blonde against the faded brown of my pillows.

It was pretty cold. The little space heater I had, my only source of warmth, had a timer that cut it off every two hours. There was no telling what time we had gotten to bed, but it had clearly been longer than two hours earlier. So, sticking my arm out from beneath the covers, I reached around blindly till I found its switch and cut it on. My hand brushed against Horace, who was curled up in his little dog bed I'd gotten him from the Christian Mission.

It wouldn't take the small heater long to warm up my "house" to a livable temperature, so until such point, I decided to continue lying in bed. I really had to pee, but that need had not yet beaten out my desire for warmth. So instead I snuggled up there next to Anna, discovering two delightful facts. One, that she was quite warm. Second, that she was quite naked.

We decided, once I had woken her, that there were other ways to warm up than waiting on the heater.

A Quest Is Embarked Upon

An hour later we were feeling right. Humming right along, you could say, bathed in a glorious green glow. At least that's how it seemed to me. The little giggle fits that Anna kept having led me to believe she was in a similar sort of mindset.

It had finally warmed up to the point that we could risk leaving the bed long enough to put our clothes on. My phone told me it was close to noon, which was echoed by a low growl that came from Anna's stomach. She was a thin little thing, but God, could she eat. I suspected the paltry Pop-Tart selection that currently constituted my food stores would not suffice.

Anna was tugging on her jeans, having already pulled on a long-sleeved black shirt with some indecipherable band logo across the chest. I stood in front of the heater warming my socks while I got up the nerve to put my feet inside what were sure to be cold shoes. I watched as she fastened her belt. "Waffle House?"

"I could live with that," she said. "Long as we don't get too crazy with it. I don't get paid till next Thursday."

Seeing her there, in all her too-tall prettiness, I was reminded that I had intended to treat her to a date this weekend. Last night, what I could remember, had just been riding around, drinking and drugging. That wasn't a date; that was everyday living.

I had sold that bit of copper and borrowed Jimmy's truck so I could steal a few deer stands I had spotted a while back. My rent was only a month behind, and I was fairly well sorted for substances to fill my little box of oblivion. I, of course, could always use more, but, well, I had enough to last me a week or so.

"On me this time," I said, pulling on shoes with teeth gritted in anticipation of the cold.

She arched an eyebrow. "Mr. Marsh, what's the special occasion?"

I thought for a moment. She always paid—for everything 'cept drugs, that is—which wasn't exactly fair. But then I never really wanted "fair" to become a precedent. I liked her—a lot, in fact—but it never pays to get folks' standards up too high.

"Let's call it an anniversary date. Or birthday. 'Cause like as not, I'll forget any sort of important date."

"Did you happen to get me a present?" she asked, a smirk crossing her face.

"Well, no, not as such, I suppose," I said.

"Then anniversary date it is." Laughing, she rose to her feet, leaned down, and kissed me. "Happy anniversary, Howard."

"Yeah, yeah." I had no idea how long we had been dating exactly, so hell, it could have been some sort of anniversary. Taking time to light a cigarette first, I walked over to the roll-up door and gave it a tug up.

A wall of cold air hit me, chased into my shed by a fairly strong breeze. "Fuck!" I yelled as it cut through my jeans and too-thin shirt. "Toss me my coat."

Anna scooped up the worn, green fatigue jacket from the back of my chair, handing it to me as she stepped out into the sunlight. She, of course, had put on a nice fleece hoodie that looked mighty warm. I just shrugged into my coat and called to Horace. "Come on."

The fat possum waddled up to me and looked up. He had a hangdog look on his face, making it clear what he thought about being out in the cold. "Move," I ordered.

He started making his way toward the dumpster, pausing by Anna to get a few quick scratches behind the ear. The cold front that had blown in overnight was no joke, but the damn critter was fat as hell, was wearing a built-in fur coat, and lived off ice cream. He'd be ok till we got back.

I turned and headed for her car. The back panel was still dented up from our first little adventure. She had claimed to the insurance company that a deer had done the damage, but even still her deductible was going to be five hundred, so dented it stayed. My uncle HD had beat it out with a hammer as best he could for her, which I thought was nice of him. You could still see it plain as day, though.

We just ignored it. I had a suspicion it was a bit of a sore subject, and I am prone to poking the bear on occasion. But I had figured she thought it was at least partially my fault that jacked-up satyr took a disliking to her car, so I kept fairly mum. It was hard at times, but what can ya do.

Climbing inside, she cranked the car and turned up the heater to full blast. She was weird in that she wouldn't drive until the heater started blowing hot air, so we sat there for a few minutes waiting for the engine to warm. I smoked my cigarette, she scrolled through Facebook on her phone. You couldn't get good service in my shed.

Finally, she was sufficiently thawed for us to embark. "So, Waffle House?" she asked.

"Lessen you wanna drive to Montgomery and go to IHOP. I just have a powerful hankering for some greasy hash browns." I hadn't told her I planned on us doing some more stuff, like maybe catch a movie, just yet. I wanted to dribble that out over the course of the day. So IHOP would get us in the right direction, but either would work, really.

She mulled it over for a second, then slipped the car in drive. "Let's do the Awful Waffle. It's closer and I'm hungry as hell."

The car crunched over the gravel lot of the storage unit, and then we were off.

I Never Saw a Purple Car

We always tended to take the more scenic routes to get places. Roads less likely to be traveled by cops. I mean, we didn't have anything really heavy on us, but a little green and a few pills can get you in a world of trouble if you aren't careful. Anna was smart about stuff like that—smarter than me, as my arrest record will inform you at length.

It was a good day, nice and pretty with a nice bit of sunshine. Had it not been so cold, we could have rode with the windows down and it would have been just perfect. So we toodled along, my eyes drifting over the countryside as some ASG came on over the CD player.

I had always thought Jubal County was the most beautiful place on earth. Not a lot of folks would agree with me, I suppose. But I could see past all the rusted cars and abandoned trailers to what lay beneath. Sure, everything was dead but the pine trees, it being winter and all, but it was still there. Brown and gray can be right pretty when you look at it in the right light.

And then I spotted that purple car.

"Stop the car!" I shouted. I will admit, I may have been a bit excited and perhaps reacted a bit too strong. I may have begun to frantically slap the dash, pushing against my seatbelt as I turned to keep facing out the side window. But in truth, I was excited.

Anna freaked a bit, slamming on the breaks. "What the fuck?"

Luckily there were no other cars in the road, so we sat there stopped across from a mostly empty field. It would be completely empty if not for the purple car parked right in the middle of it.

"Do you see that car?" I asked, pointing toward it.

"Huh, yeah. Weird place to leave a car." She paused for a second, then slapped my arm. "But what's the point? You scared the crap out of me."

I batted her arm away lightly. "The point is every time I see that car, I think about how weird it is. And how I should check it out. But the moment it gets out of sight, I forget all about it. Like the exact moment. And then I see it again and think about how weird it is I keep forgetting it."

"Howard, it's just a car."

I just kept staring at that car. "There is something going on. I'm investigating."

Before she could say anything I was out the car and walking through the ditch toward the fence line. It was three strands of barbed wire, brown with rust, hanging from half-rotted fence posts. A few trees dotted the row; the wire having been grown around in a few places.

I was pretty sure I heard a muffled "Damn it, Marsh" coming from behind me as she went to park the car on the roadside. I thought about waiting, but in truth it was probably best I went along first, just to make sure it was safe. She could catch up, and with those long legs of hers it wouldn't take her long.

Look, to be fair, I can't really blame her for being annoyed. When I hit the drugs pretty heavy I am, perhaps, prone to little flights of fancy, to perhaps tear off on wild goose chases. So, maybe she might have had reason to think this was all some weird acid flashback or something. And, yeah, I could have tried to explain that it wasn't . . . but fuck me, I had better things to do.

Easing through the barbed wire, I pulled at its slack to give me room enough to duck between the top two strands. My coat caught on the top wire, but I tugged it loose without ripping it too badly. Once I was free I trotted through the knee high grass until I was about twenty feet away from the car.

I am no good with colors, really, but it looked to me to be almost the exact same shade as a Grapico can. It looked as though it might have once had some sort of rims, and maybe some big decals. Hell, for all I know they could have once been Grapico decals! I'd once seen a car all done up with Skittles logos in Montgomery—this could have been something similar.

The closer I got, the more I knew I was right. There was some sort of hoodoo going on here. The feeling of it was thick in the air if you knew what to look for, all clammy and oozing. Muttering a few words under my breath, I felt a little tingle of Power flow out of me toward the car, a tiny ball of green energy no bigger or brighter than a lightning bug. It coursed across the distance and slowly circled the automobile.

As it passed, sigils and wards began to glow down the length of the car. They pulsed a faint blue before fading back to invisibility, but I was able to see enough to know I had no real idea what was going on here. Someone had put a whole host of spells I didn't recognize on just about every available inch of the machine, then left it in a pasture in the middle of nowhere.

It certainly had me confused.

By this time a much-annoyed Anna had traipsed up. She's a grumpy sort when she hasn't been fed, I've found. And the large rip in that nice fleece of hers likely was not helping matters much.

"It's a car, Marsh."

Everyone calls me Marsh when they are pissed. Never Howard. And as folks in my presence are usually pissed for some reason, I feel like Marsh is more my name sometimes than Howard, even though they should theoretically be equal.

"You are not wrong," I said, fairly deep in thought. "You are also not completely right. This here is bespelled."

"Bespelled?"

I leaned closer to the vehicle. "Hexed, cursed, ensorcelled. Bespelled. Someone has spent a long time making this car this way, and I aim to find out why."

I looked over to Anna. She was standing there, biting her bottom lip. More chewing it, really. "Is it safe?" she asked. The huge dent in her car went unmentioned, but it was certainly written large across her face.

"Well it ain't hurt us yet, so likely. But I ain't rightly sure what all is going on here. I'm not much of one for glyphs and wards. But I know someone who is . . ."

I pulled out my phone and hit the first number on my speed dial. It rang a half dozen times before someone picked up.

"Uncle HD? I got something I think you need to come take a look at."

THE EXPERT

A half hour later my favorite uncle, Hubert Dale, pulled his tired old van in behind Anna's car. Anna was currently sitting nearby, reading a book. She had taken the news well that we might be there a while and had promptly made her way to her trunk and got out some school books to look over. I imagine it helped that she'd found a couple of granola bars in her school bag. Not that she offered me one, you might note.

I meanwhile had just sat there staring at the car, occasionally sending my little magic-sniffing orb to slowly circle it. It was something to do while I waited. Needless to say, I was more than ready when HD made his grand appearance.

Gaunt as ever, he had his shoulder-length gray hair pulled back in a ponytail that bobbed in time to his languid stroll. He made it through the fence without catching his clothes on the wire I noted. That seemed right; HD just sorta flowed through life, slow and easy. He didn't give no trouble, and rarely did any come his way. Which is fairly rare for anyone from the Marsh Clan.

He lit a cigarette as he walked up, scratching his scraggly beard as he started eyeing the car up. "Hey, boy," he said by way of greeting, not really looking my way. He looked tired, his eyes darkly rimmed as if he had been without sleep a few days.

"You alright there, HD? You look like shit."

The man sighed, looking at me directly for the first time. "Long story. But Krista went storming up to your granny's. So you can imagine how that's going."

My heart skipped a beat. Krista was my Uncle Raymond's daughter and thus my cousin. She was really more of a sister, though, and we'd always sorta clung to each other in the bad times. I hadn't seen her in a couple of weeks though.

"Shit, I should—" I started.

"You should focus on the task at hand, and leave the rest to those of us who can do some good," snapped my uncle. It had been years since he had lost his temper at me for no good reason, so clearly things were not going well. I decided to let it lie for now.

"Fair enough," I said, raising my hands like a martyr. "Anyway, thought this might be a bit more up your alley than mine. Seeing as you can read and all." I can read of course, but not the myriad of glyphs and sigils that made up our craft. I was more of a natural savant, you could say. HD, on the other hand, couldn't cast a spell, but couldn't no one better read or write wards and such—I mean, no one who would talk to me, at least.

I brought my little orb out and started moving it slowly around. The man eased his way around, looking at all angles. He was so full of *hmmm*s and *ahhhh*s that they just kept spilling out of him left and right. It was enough to get on a body's nerves. I managed, with not insignificant effort, to keep my mouth shut, though. I really am a saint sometimes.

While he looked, I thought about Krista. I would have to go up there and see her. Though I had managed to stay out of Granny's way for well over a year now, I would risk that old biddy's wrath to check in with my cousin. I owed her that much.

HD popped up on the far side of the car. "Well now. Quite a little deal you've got here, boy."

I sidled up beside him, following his gaze. "Oh yeah?"

He gestured to the car. "Yeah. Lots going on here, but none of it's big magic. Whoever we are dealing with here, they know what they are doing, I reckon, but they don't have the juice to get it done in any hurry. They are more like me than like you, I suspect."

I nodded, mostly catching his drift.

"This, and this," he pointed to two sigils, "those mask the thing from sight. If not for you having your own magic, you would never have seen it. As it was, they made you forget about it as quick as they could."

"Well what's it hiding, then? There a dead body in the trunk or something?"

HD shook his head. "There may be, but that ain't the point of all this. In fact, if I had to guess, there are probably a few dead animals scattered around, but they are the fuel, not the purpose, if you read me." He spat. Blood magic was a thing, I knew, but no one legit would ever mess with it. Not even Granny—least not so far as I knew.

"No, you see these along here?" he gestured to a long string of the blue symbols. "These gather up magical energy. And the big one on the hood, if I am reading it right, it causes engine failure."

I looked to the hood. Etched across it was the largest of the symbols, a highly intricate glyph with a dozen smaller sigils worked into it. Far beyond anything I could ever dream of doing. "So it killed this car's engine. Seems a waste."

He looked at me blankly then, a tired, impatient look. "No, it kills *other* cars' engines. Whenever the small sigils gather up enough power, that big glyph on the front kills the engine of the next car that comes by. From my best guess, I would say maybe once or twice a week at most."

"That sounds really fucking complex, if I'm being honest. Like, way more complex than I thought glyphs could get." I really should have been studying in my downtime, but my drugs weren't going to do themselves.

HD nodded. "It's really not as complex as you think. Basically that same setup put over a . . . hell, I don't know. I can't think of an example really. But the glyph is just a general glyph for stopping stuff. It's where and what it's placed on that gives it direction and meaning. That make sense?"

"Sure," I lied. I looked from him to the car and back again. I had a lot more information now, but it still didn't make any sense. "But why?"

HD shrugged. "That's on you. I can tell you that whoever did this, I am betting they got a really good grimoire from somewhere, but no one ever taught them nothing. Anyone who had any knowhow could have told them a half dozen ways to make this better. Hell, just by turning the car to face west would have like as not made it twice as fast."

"That is some fucked up feng shui, old man."

"It is. And I ain't got a fucking clue who local would pull something like this, or why. My guess is someone off the family's radar. Maybe some stupid fucking kids or something." The man was in a powerful angry mood, and the longer he talked the more it showed. I was ready to send him on his way.

I put a hand on his shoulder. It was awkward, but then I ain't no real good at being comforting. "All right. I'll poke around a bit, I reckon, see what I turn up. I appreciate the help."

He shrugged and started for his van. "You know what to do?"

I nodded.

"Alright. I'll tell Ma about it." He took a few more steps, then paused. "You want my advice, you ask the Hog of the Road. He'll know what this is all about."

It was a smart call, even if I didn't much like the idea of it. "I may," I said to his back. "And HD, tell Krista I'll be thinking 'bout her."

All I got for my kind words was a sour look and a warning to keep my distance.

I let him go and started twirling my fingers and muttering a few words. I still had some juice left from all the partying I did the night before, and I felt it tingle its way down my fingers.

And then the car crumpled into a cube about half the size it had been a moment before. It made a horrific screeching sound as the metal collapsed in on itself, followed by a series of pops as those sigils all came undone. It was like a little fireworks show, only waist-high. It actually plum made my day. I was real shit at sigils, but making them collapse in on themselves—well, that I could handle no problem so long as I'd had plenty of time to study them, like I had here. It was basically just fucking shit up, and fucking shit up was what I was best at.

By the time I made it back into Anna's car I was humming, I was feeling so good. "To IHOP, Jeeves, and don't spare the horses!" I called, giving the dash a slap. "If we're gonna be late to food, may as well be even later! Yeah!"

Anna looked at me nonplussed for a moment, then gave a snort and her face broke into a smile. She put the car in drive and started to roll onto the roadway. "You're a weird little shit, Howard."

Which I thought was perhaps a bit harsh, even if she was not wrong.

Then she reached over and grabbed my hand. "Good thing I love you."

The girl had character, I will give her that.

That's when I saw the cross.

Blue Moon

I had paid for our late lunch when I decided to tell Anna that I was gonna spring for us to see a movie. So, we made our way up into Montgomery and hit up the cheapo matinee. I got real lucky there—we only barely made it in time for the cheap prices. Under ten bucks for both of us to see a movie? That's exactly my speed. I was maybe a touch too high to fully enjoy the more subtle nuances of the movie, but the explosions and shit were just right.

I didn't really care what we did at this point so long as Anna was happy. I just wanted us to kill time until it was dark so that then we could go back to that cross and see what really happened. Anna was more excited about it than I was, I think, when I told her, which helped. I didn't want her getting too deep in my world, but the fact she didn't run screaming from it like most folks would was a refreshing change of pace.

And so it was about six hours after we had left the purple car that I found myself back there.

Anna parked the car on the side of the road once more, her headlights falling on the small wooden cross. We sat there in the car a moment, staring at it, before I asked her to kill the lights. She turned off the car, but we just kept sitting there for a bit. I think she was waiting on me. Me, I was trying to get my mind right to face the cold.

Stepping out of the warm car was a trial, but I suffered through it. I quickly shut the door in hopes that I wouldn't let out too much warmth. I wanted to be able to dive right back in real quick like and have it still be warm inside.

There was a little wind blowing, and it was fairly overcast, but it wasn't too unpleasant of a night. If it had been warmer it would actually have been damn nice, but as it was I could feel the cold start to seep into me, threading down to my bones. If it was over forty, I would eat my coat.

Anna caught up with a little jog, and so it was that the two of us came up to the cross side by side. It was too cold to hold her hand, but I did sorta huddle close by in hopes of leeching a little warmth. We were both too skinny, me from drugs and her from height, so I knew in a minute or two we'd both be shivering like tiny little dogs. I just was counting on her height to shield me from the wind.

The cross itself was a simple affair, just two boards nailed into a four-foot T and painted white. It had then been nailed onto the side of an old oak, one that if you looked close at you could see the faint hint of old, charred bark. Almost as if a car had hit that tree at some point and caught fire.

Fifty yards away, a car that killed engines had been lying in wait, and here someone had died smacking into a tree. Had all that work, all them sigils and glyphs, had they been made up as a murder weapon? It was certainly looking that way.

The cross had the name Debra Reynolds painted on it as well as a pair of dates. Debra had only been twenty-six when she died, it looked like, assuming my math was right, which was no sure thing. She'd been loved, too, from the looks of things. There was a goodly pile of fake flowers and the like dotting the ground surrounding the cross, and you could tell that even though the death had happened years ago, folks were still bringing out stuff fresh and keeping it clean.

All I needed was the second date to work my little magic. That, and I needed a little of the luck that had so evaded Debra: I needed the wreck to have happened at night. My little moon divination only showed me things that occurred after dark, so if this had been a daytime wreck I would have to try something else. Maybe HD's suggestion of the Hog.

This was not the first time Anna would see me do magic, but it was the first time that we were both sober while it was happening. Well, mostly sober. It was also the most extravagant spell I would have done in her presence. I glanced her way out of the corner of my eye. "You ready?" I asked.

"Yeah," she said, the word coming out in a little puff of breath.

I cocked my head, listening. Other than the sound of the wind in the limbs above us, there was virtually no sound. Mostly I was listening for oncoming cars, as it wouldn't do to cause a wreck while investigating the cause of a wreck. Hearing nothing, I began to picture the date in my mind and roughly what I thought might have happened, then started to twirl my fingers.

Feeling the Power flow from my chest down my arms I closed my eyes tight, thinking hard. I just pictured a car slamming into the tree over and over, repeating the date in my mind. I stopped when I heard a sharp intake of breath beside me.

Opening my eyes, I saw the silvery outline of a compact car passing through us. Anna had jumped, but other than a faint shiver running up my spine, there was no feeling associated with the spectral car. Turning, I saw it crash into the tree, crushing the front end like an accordion.

Luckily, due to the angle, I couldn't see whoever was driving or what happened to them.

One thing was clear, though—that car had been going at a pretty high speed. Faster than a car with a dead engine should have been going. I looked off up the road and started the vision over. As I watched a silvery outline of a deer appeared, walking across the road. I saw it stop, head going up and staring into thin wisps of spectral light.

My daddy was a terror. Still is. But he always taught me that if your choice is to hit the deer or swerve off the road, always hit the deer. Deer give. Trees don't. I don't guess anyone ever taught Debra that.

Damn.

The Hog of the Road

"**Y**ou are not going to stay in the car, are you?" I asked.

Polishing off the last of a Pop-Tart, I sat in the passenger side of Anna's car. The vehicle was parked at a dirt crossroads, not too terribly far away from my family's place. The kind of dirt road I knew would like as not be deserted, which I needed for what I was about to pull.

"Correct," Anna responded as she finished rolling the joint. "You said it wasn't dangerous, just like last night, so I want to see. So we are gonna smoke this while you tell me the plan. Then we are going to do what needs doing. Need to get it wrapped up before this afternoon, because your weird magic stuff is not on my game plan. Getting fucked and fucked up, though, is."

I huffed a bit, but in truth so long as she did what I said, she really was in no danger. "Understand I voice a general objection to your attendance," I said in my most senatorial voice.

She handed me the joint and ran her now free hand across my crotch, lingering in all the right places. "Noted. And ignored," she replied, breathing out a cloud of smoke.

"Fair," I coughed around the joint a few moments later.

"So what's the deal here?" she asked as I finished my toke and passed it back to her. "What's the plan of attack?"

I shook my head. "No attack. Just gotta talk to the Hog of the Road. He should know what the story on that car back there is."

"What's that? The hog thing?" she asked.

"You know that story in the Bible where Jesus drives those demons outta that guy, and they go into a herd of pigs nearby? A herd that promptly runs itself right off into a lake or some such?"

Anna nodded. "Been a few years since I went to church, but I remember the gist of it."

"Good deal. Well the Hog of the Road, he claims to be one of them pigs. Or all of them pigs—I ain't real sure. Still got that demon inside him. And somewhere along the way, he decided to take an interest in roads. I say he, but again, really it could be *hogs*, plural. I ain't really sure. But he, or them—they know about anything you need to know about roads, if you know how to ask. But then most any crossroads demon can, if you have the right handle on them. Or the right offering."

"You realize how insane it is that we are having this conversation, right?" she asked.

"I have a hint, yeah. Though I've been dealing with this shit my whole life, so it's only a little insane to me."

"And can we do this in broad daylight? Doesn't it need to be nighttime or something? Midnight, maybe?"

I chuckled. "Nope. I mean, most times you only do stuff like this in the dark so as folks won't see you. Here, we can hear a car coming from miles off, so no need to worry about getting spotted." I glanced into the back seat. Horace was back there curled up asleep in a cat carrier, there in case of emergency.

She leaned back, breathing in a lungful of smoke. "Never a dull moment with you." She offered me the last hit but I passed. I needed to be at least a little sharp for this. I waited on her to finish it off and then stepped out of the car.

"Grab those salt shakers out your purse!" I called over my shoulder.

I didn't see the confusion that surely came over her face. It was quite the battle, really. Look and be amused, or play it cool and just keep walking.

"What salt shakers?" she yelled from inside the car. Then a moment later, "Damn it, Marsh!"

I had stolen a few salt shakers from IHOP yesterday and put them in her purse.

When I heard her car door slam I finally looked. She had a trio of salt shakers in her hand. "Now I have salt all in my purse, you ass."

That was no good. "Damn, maybe I shoulda grabbed a couple more. I didn't account for spillage."

She stared at me then with one of the weirdest looks I have ever seen. It was a look of barely restrained mayhem but with an undercurrent of abject wonderment. I couldn't much fathom what that was all about, so I just stepped over and grabbed the trio of items from her hands. I held them up, looking at each in turn. They were, on average, about eighty percent full. "This will do, I reckon. In a pinch."

I chuckled at my pun.

I think her eye twitched, but I was too busy scoping out the shakers to pay her much mind.

So I just ignored whatever it was she had going on and set about my rat killin'. I went to the center of the crossroads and drew a circle in the dirt with a stick. I made it big enough for the two of us to step inside, then set about putting a trickle of salt in the gash I had made. As I worked, I wondered how best to work in a salt pork pun into the conversation, but my weed-dulled mind wasn't having it at the moment.

Thankfully there was just enough salt to finish. My work done, I stepped into the circle and waved Anna over. There was a bit of hesitation there, but she came. I had made the circle a touch on the small side, I found, so we had to stand there mighty close together. I will admit I was not much opposed to that at all, but there were more important matters at hand.

Facing outwards, I said a few words in a language fairly well forgotten by most of the modern world. It rolled off my tongue with well-worn practice, flowing like smooth honey. I could feel damn near the last dregs of what Power I had pass through me, forcing those words out into the ether. There were other ways to call the Hog up, but my way was safest, I reckoned.

And then nothing happened.

I stood there a minute in silence, waiting for the demon to appear. It had never taken this long before.

"Is it coming?" whispered Anna.

I gave a little shrug. "Never failed before. I'mma try again."

I repeated the words, making double sure I said every syllable perfectly correct. This time the absolute last snippet of my Power was drained, leaving me feeling all out of sorts. But the words had been said. The Hog of the Road would come.

And then the overpowering smell of barbeque filled my nostrils. It was so strong I could have been standing inside a smokehouse. You could even taste the smoke on the air, even though there was no smoke visible.

"Son of a bitch!" I kicked a break in the salt circle as I stormed back toward the car.

"Howard?" called Anna.

I put my hand on the car door and looked back at her. "I hope you're hungry again. 'Cause we need to go get some barbeque. But first, I need drugs. *Lots* of drugs."

PREACH'S PIT

I was humming right along now. A quick stop by my shed had me full to the gills, and now I couldn't sit still hardly. I knew Anna wasn't real big on my little glass pipe goodies, but she hadn't said anything. She just took a couple of her favorite pills and waited in the car while I handled my business. I would make it up to her later that night, I was sure. Or maybe I wouldn't. But I at least had the general intention of making it up to her. I knew I had a little bit of goodwill built up from our surprise date, so maybe I would play it a little loose and see.

It was with no small amount of reticence that we pulled up to Preach's Pit, the finest barbeque joint in Jubal County, if not the world. Under the careful ministrations of Preston "Preach" Barrett, six days a week delicious piles of meat flowed into the stomachs of the county's more discerning foodies. But this being Sunday, sadly, they weren't open. So there was only a pair of cars off to one side, back where the employees parked, one of which I knew would belong to Preach himself. So it was that I made my way toward the cinderblock building that was the restaurant proper from where we parked.

It had been painted yellow once, but the sun had faded it to a more of a bone color. A big mural of a cross was on the left side of the screen door, while to the right side of it was a dancing pig wearing a bowler hat. Both were as faded as the rest of the building, but they stood out nonetheless. And there, perched on its tin roof, was the dark wooden sign with wood-burned letters that read PIT B-B-Q.

Looking around, I could see the small church that was Preach's job on the days he wasn't cooking up barbeque about a hundred yards off to the left, set back in an oak grove. The Elk Grove AME Church had seen better days, most of its members having moved over to the larger Sumpville congregation and its fancy new building. Every Sunday, however, the Preach traded the pit for the pulpit, following in his daddy's shoes. It being later in the afternoon, its parking lot was empty. Service would have ended at least an hour or two earlier, I reckoned.

Anna had wanted to come with, of course, but I managed to talk her into waiting in the car. I didn't think it would be dangerous—Preach and I were on somewhat decent terms—but she was important enough that I was going to play it safe. If they had been open, I would have had her see about scoring us some pulled pork, but as usual

Jubal County's preoccupation with religion was working to my detriment.

With her safely out of the way, I made my way around to the back of the building. The smells of slow-cooking pork hit me before I ever came in sight of the above-ground pits they used to prepare the meat, and just that quick my mouth was watering. Rounding the corner I saw the three tin-covered cinderblock pits, each with good-smelling smoke rising up from within. Good pork takes many hours to cook, so many that Preach had to get started the Sunday afternoon before to make sure it would be ready come Monday.

It's why his congregation didn't have Sunday evening service, which was another draw that Sumpville AME had over his church. To my mind this should have been his biggest draw of all, as the less church, the better, to my mind. But some folks, they just couldn't get enough of it, more's the pity.

What I sought, though, was the shed behind the pits. The shed where Preach butchered the hogs himself.

It was a small building, hardly a dozen feet across and maybe that deep. Nothing but some old wooden slats and a few bits of rusted tin, long turned brown under the elements. Even if you didn't know what went on inside, it had a creepy vibe. Death clung hard to that place, even if it didn't have quite the charnel smell you'd expect of a place where a hog or two a day might meet their end.

Walking up, I rapped the door with the back of my hand. "Preach?"

Inside I heard what sounded like a muffled curse. "That you, Marsh?"

"You know it."

The voice was deep, rumbling through the thin wooden wall. "Go away, then, I ain't got time for you today."

My patience was worn pretty thin. I am not one to enjoy a bunch of running around all day; I much prefer to loiter in one place at length, and I had had precious little of that today. "Preach, I ain't got time to be fucking around. I think I know what you got going on in there, just let me in so I can have a few words."

I swear the man growled. "God as my witness, you come through that door, I'm gonna brain you good."

"That ain't very Christian of you, now," I said, getting steadily more pissed.

I could hear him moving around in there, and I was pretty sure I heard a blade getting stopped against leather, being sharpened. That wasn't a very inviting sound. "Good thing God forgives then ain't it. Now go on, git."

I took to pounding on the door a bit, causing the door to rattle in the frame. I could almost sort of see through the cracks, and what I could see looked like a bloody mess. There was a pig getting butchered, that was for sure. "Goddamn it, Preach! You're fucking around with the Hog, and ain't nothing good going to come from that!"

That door came flying open, and I wasn't even close to being ready. The wood of the door smacked me right in the face with enough force to send me falling back on my ass. It got me more on the chin than the nose, thank God, but it still hurt like all hell and I flirted with blacking out, I think. Lucky me, the pain was bad enough to keep me conscious. I could feel blood coming down from where the skin had split under the force of it.

Preach loomed over me, damn near blocking out the sun as he went to help me up. "Marsh, I'd apologize but you know what I told you 'bout using the Lord's name like that. Come up in here, causin' a ruckus like that—you know better. I know for a fact your Granny taught you better."

"For a fact she did *not*," I said, taking his much larger hand. It was so big it totally engulfed my own as he started to pull me to my feet. "Old bitch never taught me anything, you know that."

He dropped me. "I also done told you about honoring your elders. You're just bound and determined to get on my bad side today, ain't you, Marsh?"

With that, he turned and went back inside, leaving me to get myself up. My chin was dripping blood onto my shirt, and once I was on my feet I tried to cup my hands under it to catch as much as possible. Still in a fair bit of pain, I followed in after.

It was gloomy inside. The single light that dangled overhead was yellowed with age and flickered ominously. It left the room shadowy around the edges, and it was in one of these shadows that the big man was moving to take a seat in. The metal chair groaned under his weight, but he didn't so much as bat an eye.

Preach was tall, taller even than Anna. So tall that seated as he was in that metal folding chair, he looked me in the eye. He was broad, too, easily weighing over 350 lbs. There was fat there, of course, but muscle too. Covering him was a stained apron splattered with dark crimson, and in his large hands he was back to sharpening a knife.

Off to one side there were a couple of massive deep freezers where he stored his cut meet, no doubt. The center of the room was taken up by a metal table, though, and that's where my eyes went. On it lay the dressed carcass of a massive hog, laid out to drain all the blood, which was catching in a bucket set to one end.

Preach eyed me warily. "Grab one of them paper towels for your chin, then tell me whatcha want, Marsh. I ain't got all day either."

"He came to see me," came a raspy voice.

On the table, the head of the boar lifted and turned to face me. Its eyes were as dead as the rest of it, and even though it spoke, its jaw did not move. Not that it had lungs with which to make a sound anyway. "Hello, Howard Marsh. I heard you calling, but as you can see, I am a bit indisposed at the moment."

I looked over at Preach. "Really?"

The big man shrugged. "It don't mind, and hog prices keep going up. Gotta save money somehows."

"I really don't mind," said the Hog of the Road. There was a hint of humor in its voice, as if it found all this to be just the biggest laugh. That wasn't a good sign, I reckoned.

"I bet you don't. I don't even want to know what you get out of this, but I know it's something." *I really should tell Granny about this*, I thought. I had my doubts she would approve, but I decided to just keep on. "Look, I don't care what you two do behind closed doors. Well, I mean I do, just not right now . . . I mean this is properly fucked up. Fuck."

I was a bit out of sorts, and the pain in my chin wasn't helping. I could see that I was soaking through this paper towel mighty quick and went ahead and grabbed a couple more from the roll. This was not going as expected. I had thought Preach would just be talking to the Hog, maybe getting sermon material or something. Not turning it into a couple racks of ribs and some chops.

This just confirmed my belief that those who can do magic should avoid conventional jobs, like running a restaurant. Leave a hoodoo master like Preach in charge of a pork joint, and he summons a demon pig to butcher to save on costs. Tomorrow we would probably have a dozen folks running around possessed or something.

That was Preach's problem, though. He was the second most powerful spell slinger in the county, so whatever.

That grating, raspy voice burrowed monotonously into my head. "Howard Marsh, don't be so out of sorts. I will help you sometime when my body has had time to reform."

That would not do. I was too hopped up to take a no. "Nope, help me now. All I need to know is who set up that car-wrecking sigil car thingy over near Edgar Thomas's place."

A muted laugh came from the gaping chest of the dressed hog. "I am busy now, Howard Marsh. Leave me be."

I looked over at Preach. That man had summoned the pig up. He could compel it.

"You heard what the demon said," Preach said, coming to his feet once more, that too large knife bared in his hand. I took a step back, but the man just started sawing at the hog carcass. The Hog made little giggling noises as he cut, which was truly fucked up.

I was mad. "How the hell you gonna take a demon's side over mine? Ain't that against your code or something? What kind of preacher are you?"

He didn't look up from his work. "The kind of preacher with a failing church and a struggling business that needs money to sink back into them so I can turn things around. If it helps me do God's work, then I'll do whatever it takes. I got half a dozen employees and three times that in the congregation that are all looking to me. So either lend a hand, or get up out my way. 'Cause I figure each week I cut up this here hog, that's a couple hundred bucks or more I just saved. Can do a lot of good with that."

"A lot of good," giggled the Hog.

Preach smacked that carcass upside it's head. "You hush."

I looked from the dead demon pig back to the mountain of a man butchering it. How was it I was the only sane one in this room? "I . . ." I was at a loss for words. For once in my fucking life I couldn't think of a response.

Preach gestured to the open door. "Go on now, and try again later. I'll have what I need come tomorrow night, so round about Tuesday he's all yours."

"Be seeing you, Howard Marsh," came that lilting voice from behind those cold, dead eyes.

I sort of staggered out of there, a good bit bewildered. I think that between my head getting rocked back and the way too many drugs I had taken in anticipation of facing off with the Hog of the Road, my mind was fried. I just did what I was told, without so much as another peep.

I mean I stole the roll of paper towels, but other than that I didn't even argue. I just tucked tail and ran, so to speak. Not that I could have really fought too much. Preach was second only to Granny, far as I knew, and even with my usual cocktail of "overcooking my body with drugs so my magic is somewhat usable" he would very likely wipe the floor with me.

That said, I did pause and spend a bit too long thinking about setting that damn shed on fire. I ain't a murderer, but right then it was mighty tempting. My chin was pulsing in pain, my shirt was ruined, and I could just feel the headache starting to blossom behind my eyes. And having to explain all this to Anna . . .

Fuck.

I could tell I was crashing, spiraling down fast. Not that I was any less hyped from drugs, but my mood was quickly downshifting, and I knew that before too much longer I wouldn't be worth a damn as I just moped the rest of the day away.

Wadding up a double handful of paper towels, I dropped the blood-soaked ones from my chin and jammed the clean ones tight against my skin. It hurt like the devil, but I was sinking and didn't even care. I just wanted to go crawl into my shed and go to sleep, if the drugs would let me.

Before I reached Anna's car she climbed out and came running up. I guess she saw me in the rearview and could tell I'd got hurt. And she took to doing what she did best: nursing my hurt.

I was still powerfully messed up in the head, and I may have started bawling, but damn if she didn't have a way to soothe the inside hurts as well as the outside.

She cared, without reservation.

I hadn't known how starved for that I was.

DELIVERANCE

I t was full dark out when I had Anna drop me off a quarter mile up the road from Preach's.

The time between my earlier visit till then had been spent in perhaps not the most fun of ways. I'd had a pretty bad breakdown, even with Anna there. Depression can be a righteous bitch sometimes, and let me tell ya, the drugs don't help any. They can dull and hide the pain for a bit, but when it comes bubbling up it's all the worse for it.

A lot of tears were shed, mostly on my end. Anna was a real good sport about it, even if she did get a bit preachy at times trying to nudge me toward rehab. I mean, I'm sure it could have done some good, and I wasn't doubting that I needed it. But it just wasn't gonna happen. Not now, at least.

Between Anna, Krista, and HD I had a fuckin' Greek chorus all chirping away trying to get me help. God, it was annoying. Was I doing fine? No. Was I wanting to keep living this life? Also no. But I also wasn't gonna give up the drugs, so it was all moot.

Anna was at least less annoying about it than the other two would have been.

So yeah, tears happened, then we just sort of hung out for a bit. My shed isn't exactly a Mecca for fun activities, but we made it work. Anna sprung for us each to get a Blizzard from the Dairy Queen, and then we settled in to kill some time. That meant me failing to read a book due to being too high while she played with Horace.

I wished I could have burned off most of that high with some magic, but I knew that I might need it later. And I wasn't so flush with drugs that I was looking to do up a bunch more so soon. So, I just had to live with it. Which . . . sucked. I mean, I like being high, but being high with a purpose? Meh. Unless that purpose was forgetting or numbing, that is.

But soon enough it was dark, and she'd been kind enough to agree to take me back out to the Pit, so long as I agreed that afterwards we would have some fun. That was an easy enough promise to make, since it would just mean getting drunk and then getting into shenanigans. I'd have done that anyway. I just had to come out the other side of this little exploratory mission, was all.

I could have just let things sit. Just waited till the Hog of the Road reformed his body well enough to answer my call. But I figured I needed to move a little quicker than that. Whoever spelled up that car would figure out that it had gone to shit sooner rather than later, and I wanted to be able to hopefully get the jump on them. If I waited too long, Granny might get involved . . .

That thought left a shudder running up my spine. Damn old bat.

I had on what was basically my sneaky clothes, the stuff I would wear to steal copper and the like—black jeans and a black hoodie. Both had come off my ex Lidda's clothesline, no doubt belonging to one of her many baby daddies, which just made them feel that much better of a fit. I am a petty son of a bitch sometimes. I love it.

Preach's Pit had a bit of a cool glow to it from the moonlight, but the rest of the area was heavily bathed in shadow. I had to duck down in a ditch once thanks to a passing car, but other than that I was pretty sure there was no one around to see me. Both cars were gone from the lot, and there were none over by the church either other than a church bus with a flat tire.

Still, though, I paused for a bit, just to get a feel for things. The drugs didn't want to let me, but I fought them into line long enough for me to just be still. I couldn't like, send my senses out magically or anything, but I could try and read which way the magical wind was blowing, so to speak.

The night was cool, and the sounds of crickets were a constant background hum. The longer I stood the more noises I could pick out, like the croaking of a distant frog. There was a little bit of night breeze blowing, just enough that its cool touch on my neck had me draw up my hood over my head. That muffled the sounds a bit, but I had heard enough and, more importantly, felt enough. There was no big magic being worked that I could feel.

I skirted the tree line as far as I could, then made my way to the butcher shed. If it had been creepy looking in the day, it was fucking terrifying looking in the night, let me tell you. It was a place where death hung heavy, and as I got closer I could hear the buzzing of flies.

Taking one last look around I couldn't see anyone, and my patience for being safe was gone. I reached out and tugged on the handle. It came open with a rusted groan, revealing the darkened interior. Even with my eyes adjusted to the night, it was so pitch-black in that shed that I couldn't make out anything beyond vague shapes.

And then there were two red glowing eyes staring back at me as a low, demented laugh came from within. It was followed by a soft, lilting voice. "Hello, Howard Marsh. We have been waiting for you."

Pay (Fat) Back

My blood froze. I knew that the Hog of the Road was there; it was the whole reason I had come calling. But knowing a thing and confronting a thing in the flesh are two very different experiences sometimes. That buzzing fly sound had grown louder, and I began to suspect that there were no flies at all.

I called up that little blue bit of magic I do from time to time and used it to give me light enough to see. The pale glow had the eerie effect of letting me see but also deepening the shadows that flitted around the edges of my vision. Mostly, though, it gave me a good view of that damned hog.

It was gone from the table. Instead, it now hung from a hook in the corner of the shed. It swayed gently though I knew damn well no breeze could have touched it—not inside. And even dressed out like it was, I knew it had to be pretty damn heavy.

The hog's eyes never blinked. They just stared at me, both lifeless and somehow glowing. It was like looking into a shark's eyes, only far creepier. As the carcass swayed and slowly spun, that face never stopped looking at me, and as the body started to twist away from me I could hear the neck bones snap and crack as the Hog of the Road kept its gaze locked onto me.

"I knew you would be back, Howard Marsh. You are always so impatient. I'm growing as fast as I can." There was an odd sound in the air, almost like crackling, but . . . meaty? It was impossible to describe, but it was a sickening sound. Floating my light closer I could see that the butchered flesh was slowly regrowing, reforming around shattered bone and sliced meat. It was like watching decay in reverse, and seeing globs of fat wiggle around like maggots turned my stomach something fierce.

Before I could even think, I had to step back outside and began to empty my guts out onto the ground in a series of retches. The taste of bile was thick on my tongue as I managed to finally straighten back up a minute later, everything I had eaten in the past few days lying in a splattered pile between my feet.

Wiping my mouth with the sleeve of my hoodie, I stepped back into the doorway. "Fuck, that's disgusting."

A giggle came back. Through all this, the thing's mouth never moved, but the words still flowed out that mouth like slick honey. "So here we are," it crooned at me.

"You know what I want."

I swear those dead, red eyes winked at me. "Yes, but you didn't call and bind me, so I don't have to answer. Such a pity."

"I can send you back, though. I know enough to know how to break a binding." I figured a thing like the Hog of the Road wouldn't just let itself get used for a few racks of ribs and the like, not without having some sort of ulterior motive.

"Oh, but then our good friend Preach will be most upset, and you know good and well who he's going to blame for that. No, I don't think you will. Because I know what you are, Howard Marsh."

"And what's that?" I instantly regretted the words. Playing with bound demons was a shit idea; they couldn't hurt you in the physical, so they did everything they could to fuck your mind up.

"A coward," he hissed.

I laughed. "No shit, Sherlock. That supposed to hurt?"

There was only a split second of the sound of a chain rattling that gave me any warning.

The carcass fell to the ground, head flopping obscenely as it twisted to land on all four bloody stumps where its hooves would have been. Even as it touched down it came bounding toward me, making a hideous squelching sound with each step as flesh hit wooden slat. The eyes flared brighter, so strong that they all but overpowered my little blue light, turning the air a sickly looking purple.

A roar came from it, and finally its mouth moved. I heard neck bones snap back into place as its jaws gaped wide, revealing a pair of wicked-looking tusks. I knew damn well those could slice me right open if given half a chance, splitting me wide open for the Hog of the Road to then feast on my innards.

It came on so fast that had I not already been taking a step back, it would have gotten me. As it was, the damn thing caught a tusk on my hoodie, ripping a gouge into it. If I hadn't been so skinny it would have laid me right open. Still, that tusk catching like that almost kept me from getting all the way through the door frame.

As that tusk went to go across the space where the door would have been there was an eruption of golden sparks. The scent of charred ozone and sulfur filled my nose, causing me to gag, even as the flash of light liked to blind me. It all left me reeling, and I fell back for the second time that day.

Only this time I landed in my own puke.

The Hog of the Road was hurled back from the boundary, causing it to slam into the cutting table, knocking it on its side and breaking one of its legs. That didn't even slow the creature; it was damn near instantly back on its feet. It stalked right up to the edge of Preach's wards and just stared at me, tusks bared and waiting.

I got to my feet, not even bothering to try and clean myself up. The Hog of the Road had stopped talking, stopped giggling, and just stood there perfectly still save for the wiggling ends of its reforming flesh.

We stood there staring at each other, neither of us talking. It gave me time to chew things over, to flesh out the seeds of ideas that had been coming all afternoon. Things slotted together, and the way ol' hoggy boy was trying to scare me off sealed the deal for me.

"That meat, it's bad stuff, ain't it. Preach reckons he has a way around it, though, he ain't dumb. But you . . . you think he's gonna drop the ball somehow."

That was met with silence. And then the Hog of the Road stood up on the stumps of its back two legs and began to slowly, shudderingly, dance around the room to some unheard tune. After a few moments it began to hum, a grating sound more like growling than anything that would come out of a human. It shuffled around the room like some macabre dancing bear, weaving around the broken table.

Fucking A, it was some creepy shit.

"Don't tell me what I want to know, and I'm gonna send you back and burn that whole shed down, with all the meat in it. Tell me, and I leave things between you and Preach."

The creepy fuck just kept dancing. The humming sound was getting louder, grating on my ears like nails on a chalkboard, and through it all I still heard the buzzing of flies. It made my jaw ache, deep down in the bone.

I started to call up my Power, getting ready to sever this nightmare's connection to our world. It had been summoned, and even though I hadn't been the one to do the summoning, Preach wasn't around to stop me. It would take a lot longer—and might end up hurting me a bit—but by God, that fucker would be gone.

The Hog stopped it's prancing and slowly turned to face me. It knew that at least for a split second I would have to cross the wards Preach had built into the walls in order to sever its link. Which was dangerous, but if I did my prep right it really would take just a second. So the risk was minimal . . . probably.

"Let us discuss things, Howard Marsh."

"No discussion. Tell me, or go bye-bye."

The carcass huffed angrily, if it could be called that, then rolled its dead eyes toward me once again. "The man you seek is a tow truck driver named Arnold Brandt. Now go away, Howard Marsh. I would hate for my meat to start to go bad."

I had a name. It could be lying . . . it probably even was, or at the very least was holding something back. But it was probably about the best I was going to get. I set about marshalling my power, getting ready to sever the Hog in the Road's connection.

"What are you doing, Howard Marsh? We had a deal." There was suspicion and not a little bit of anger in its voice. There were no more giggles to be had, it seemed.

"Did we? I forget," I muttered as I focused on teasing out the magic in front of me. My blue orb was still inside the circle, sort of sniffing out the information I needed as I worked out what "thread" to snip.

"We. Had. A. DEAL!" it squealed.

I ignored it. It began to rage, flinging its carcass around the room, slamming into the table, the deep freezers, the chains in the corner. It slammed into walls, causing showers of golden sparks to rain down a welder had gone wild. It cursed and shrieked as it flailed, and with tusks bared it tried leaping futilely for me over and over. Its body was wrecked, broken bones protruding from half grown flesh, held together by hate and spite alone.

It made it hard to focus, needless to say.

Had I summoned Mr. Piggy, a snap of my fingers and it would have been gone. But this took close to ten minutes as I teased and poked and eventually slipped my grasp around the bit of magic Preach was using to keep it here. And all the while the thing cursed my name.

Honestly, it was a lot like my family get-together at Christmas, only the ham wasn't honey baked.

In the end, though, I had it, and without warning I stepped forward to slip my arm inside the wards and send the fucker back. But what had looked like the wild flailing of something mad was a bit more tactful that I thought. The moment I stepped in, the Hog in the Road lunged for me tusk first.

My hand was reaching out, fist glowing faintly with blue-red light, looking to break the connection. But the Hog was only a foot away, if that, and its mouth was set to take my arm off at the wrist. My heart stopped as I waited to feel the pain come in a split second, but somehow I managed to remember what I had to do.

I opened my fist and loosed a thought. The Hog's mouth was closing on my hand, so close I could feel hot breath and bloody, foamy spit dripping down . . .

And then it was gone.

Only the scent of blood, sulfur, and urine remained. I had pissed myself.

It matched the vomit on my ass, I guess, but needless to say I was real embarrassed. I was not looking forward to getting back into Anna's car and explaining this. So I decided there was only one thing to do, but first I needed to see something.

Walking over to the deep freezers, I opened them both, looking inside. Each was full of meat, no doubt from the Hog in the Road. I didn't know what Preach was thinking . . . holy water in the BBQ sauce? But I knew Granny would have my ass if I didn't do something.

I took off my pants and boxers, hurling them onto the remains of the table. Then I summoned up my magic, lit them on fire, and watched as the flames spread to the table, then the wood floor. When the first wall started to catch I knew I was good to go, so I struck a trot off in the direction Anna was supposed to be waiting.

The night air was cold on my ass.

I started trying to think of what I would tell Anna. And, more importantly, just how in the hell I would keep Preach from giving me an old-school biblical smiting.

That, though, was tomorrow's problem, I decided as I glanced back to see the shed totally in flames.

Take a Breath

My broke-ass recliner had rarely felt so good. I was still hopping right along on the tail end of my high, but I was home and fixed my pantsless situation. The best part was that Anna hadn't even hassled me much about the whole running bare-assed thing. She'd just checked that nothing sex crime related had happened, then just made a point of tossing me an extra jacket from her back seat and driving on.

All things considered, the day had certainly not gone the way I had intended and had gotten a bit dark, really. But now to be back home, finally able to just relax a bit . . . that was heaven. It was actually shaping up to be a little bit of a party, or at least as much of one as I ever allow. Anna was there, of course, as was Liam and his girlfriend, Marketta, who luckily was also a friend of mine. I am not really one for strangers. Lastly my neighbor Corey was making an appearance, which made me happy. His wife was still putting him through the wringer and he could use the chance to blow off some steam.

A delightful assortment of goodies were making the rounds, everyone sharing and caring. Lots of love in the room, which was nice. Helped get my mind off tomorrow, which would like as not be full of bullshit as I tracked down some bush league magic user and convinced him to lay off the shenanigans. Least until he ran it by Granny.

Anna was sitting on the arm of my recliner, making it list like a sinking ship to one side, but seeing as she didn't hardly weigh nothing despite how tall she was, I just pulled her down into my lap. She squawked a little but stopped when I took to kissing her a bit. It was her what convinced me to let it all wait till Monday.

She could have run me by this guy's shop, which she had actually heard of, whenever she got up to get back to the "real world." But I only got so much time with her each week, and who knew if the place would even be open that early? I decided to spend a bit more time with her before she got on back to her job and school and shit. We might even track down some early breakfast instead, on the square in Elk Grove. The world was our oyster. I could just hit up HD for a ride later.

Corey was telling Liam about something to do with filing taxes, really just digging into the subject as best as the drunk man could. In the meantime the girls were chatting about school, seeing as Marketta was gonna be starting up there where Anna went in the summer. Just a veritable hum of conversation.

Me, I just sat there letting it all wash over me. I was high and slowly coming down, a descent slowed by the goodies being passed. I was ripped enough that I could just about see the words flowing around the room more than I could hear them. I felt like I was in a few places at once, even though I was just a sitting still. It was glorious.

I really needed to blow off a bit of this high, though, before I did something stupid. Anna knew what was up with me, but the rest, far as I knew, had no real clue. So, slapping Anna on the ass, I nudged her up from the seat and rolled up the door just enough to step outside to go piss. Least that's what I told them as I lowered the door behind me.

It was cold, and I hadn't put my jacket on. I was pretty instantly filled with regret about that but just carried on till I reached the corner I usually pissed on. Stepping out of sight, I was protected from sight by the sheds on one side and the Dairy Queen fence on the other. I could hear Horace rummaging around in there, feasting on fresh dumpster leavings from the day's cleanup.

Leaning back against the wall to ground myself, I started twirling fingers and muttering words. Most times for an illusion I needed a picture or something—a way to refresh my mind. There was one face, though, I didn't need that help with: Krista's. Within a few moments she was standing there, flipping me the bird. Her body was spectral, as I didn't want to use up too much of my magic. I might need some later. But it didn't take much to give her an outline and to give her eyes a blue glow. She was laughing, giving her hair a shake. I hadn't realized how much I had missed her the past month or so. She was my best friend, and she seemed to be going through some shit. And, as usual, I was nowhere to be found. It was a few seconds before I realized I was crying a little. I was too fucked up to really know why, but it certainly felt right.

Then the cold got a bit much, and I felt like I had burned off enough of my high to keep me from trying to do something stupid, like a little love/sex/orgy magic or some sort of stupid, crazy illusion to impress my neighbor. I gave my head a shake, and Krista was gone.

I trotted off back to the shed, shivering pretty good. It felt mighty good once I was back in my recliner again, Anna once more across my lap, even if she was giving me a little playful grief about how long I took.

Liam tossed the two of us some beers from his cooler, which Anna caught deftly. A keeper, she was.

Life was good.

A Routine Stop

Monday

"It's been awhile since I've been down this way," Hubert Dale said.

We were bumping down Brandt Creek Road, which I thought was a bit pompous a name for what equated to basically a glorified driveway. It was fairly well maintained, I supposed—it would have to be for a wrecker to make its way up and down on the regular—but it was still a bumpy little stretch of clay.

"Oh yeah?" I muttered. I was sorta paying him attention, but not really. Mostly I was staring off into the trees that grew right up to beside the road. We were in the thick of some sort of pine plantation by the looks of things, one in bad need of thinning. It was dark under those limbs, and if it kept on it would stunt those trees.

"Yep. Few years back I was working on fixing up a car for one of my exes to drive, and we went to every junkyard in the county before all was said and done. Brandt's was one of the last we stopped at. I just ended up ordering the part online, though, since no one local seemed to have it. EBay is a wonderful thing."

I grunted in acknowledgment. The pines were putting me in a bleak mood; they had that effect. Well, not all pines, mind you. Just pine plantations like this.

A bit of silence stretched, so I opted to fill it. "I've never really dealt with shops too awful much. Not that I have any skill, mind you. Or a car, the past five years or so. But before that, Uncle Mike, he's always been a fair enough hand at *mechanicing* to do what I've needed done. So is Daddy, I reckon. So I guess I've always pretty well kept it in family. May be why's I ain't ever been out this way."

HD said something back, but my mind was lost in them pines. That wouldn't do, though, so sighing, I turned my head away to look forward. Up ahead I could see that we were approaching a gate. The road curved off to the right, going Lord knows where, but there in the middle of the curve was a chain-link fence and its open gate. A battered black mailbox leaned beside it, its mouth hanging open.

The gate was in a cut in the road bank, and I could see the drive rose gradually out of sight behind it. Along its length, least as far as I could see, were the rusted-out husks of stripped-down cars. Each had been painted some different color but so long ago that the paint had long flaked off, leaving a uniform brown shade on each. It was definitely one of the weirder fences I had ever seen.

"Brandt Towing and Yard" read a sign that looked tie wrapped to the fence. It sported a few holes, and a good bit of fade on it as well. All in all, it wasn't the most inspiring of sights, I had to admit. And I suspected that there would be little behind that fence to change my view.

My uncle nosed the car up the drive. "When I came here last time, all these cars had been painted. I thought it was weird looking, because it was all pastel colors."

"Not the most typical of manly colors, I take it?" I asked, watching the cars as we passed them by. Up close you could better see the tiny splotches of paint that remained, all pinks and yellows.

He shook his head. "Not at all. Which, when you see Mr. Brandt, doesn't make a lot of sense. He looks like a . . . like a mechanic. I ain't trying to be some sort of way about it—a guy can like whatever he likes. It just didn't fit the guy. I don't know how else to put it."

We topped the rise then and Brandt's place hovered into view.

Close by on the right was a single-wide trailer with a large porch attached to its front. A few plants and chairs dotted it, along with a covered swing that I am pretty sure I saw for sale at Walmart last summer. A little green Beetle was parked in front, the kind what had the flower hubcaps, and next to it was a blue Ford F-150 that had seen better days, from the looks of things.

Off to the left was a two-bay workshop, your typical small-time mechanic's shop. A few cars were parked in and around it in what seemed like various states of repair. A yellow-painted wrecker was parked in front of what looked to be the door to a small office or something. Brandt Towing was written large down the side of it, as if I needed any more confirmation.

Mostly what caught my eye, though, was the junkyard. From the ridge where we were driving it spread out before us, about the size of a pair of football fields. It was a good hundred yards down the hill away from the house and shop, but the entrance to it damn near split the distance about perfect between them. A chain-link fence kept it separated off, but you could see row upon row of cars filling it up. They went right up to the tree line off in the distance, pretty much.

I bet you couldn't have fit too many more cars in there without stacking them on top of one another, either. It looked just about slam-packed. They were in rows of sorts, but once you got away from the gate a bit, those rows became a right confusing-looking maze to me. If there was a center point, it would have to be this pair of tractor trailers right near the middle, which, if I had to guess, was where he stored parts.

I gave a low whistle. "Now that's a junkyard." My mind started turning at all the treasure one such as me could find out there.

"Yeah, it's a lot more full than when I came here before," said HD.

He guided the car right up to the shop. I didn't see anyone moving around, but I had my doubts the man would leave it wide open if he wasn't there. I turned to him as I unfastened my seatbelt. "Just wait in the car. I'll have quick talk with Brandt and then maybe we go track down some lunch. Sound good?"

"Fair enough," he said, giving me a little nod. Not having any real magic of his own, if things went south it would be best for him to stay out of the line of sight.

It was slightly warmer than it had been that weekend, but that meant it was still fairly cold. I pulled my jacket tight around me and stuck off toward the open bay doors. I was still feeling a bit out of sorts, but I knew the mood would likely pass soon. At least I hoped it would.

There were two cars inside, one per bay. Each had their hood up, but beyond that they looked fine enough, I thought. The space directly around each car was relatively free of clutter, but the surrounding walls were filled with all manner of junk. Tool chests stood next to stacks of worn tires, while boxes of belts were stacked atop what looked to be all manner of engine parts. A grimy calendar with some sort of Mustang with a woman draped across the hood hung near some sort of picture of a little league team.

In short, it was exactly like every other small-time mechanic's shop I had ever been in, right down to that oily mechanical smell that filled the air. It was like as not seeping up from the heavily stained concrete floor, which was almost black with old spills. It was a smell I was right fond of, actually, reminding me of my uncle's garage a bit.

To my right was a wooden door that must have led into the office. As I didn't see Mr. Brandt working on either of the cars, I figured he had to be inside there. More than likely trying to thaw out a bit. So, making my way around the bumper of a deep-blue Pontiac, I gave the door knob a twist. It opened right up.

"Sorry," said a muffled voice. "Didn't hear you come up."

Arnold Brandt Takes a Stroll

Seated behind a good-sized desk was the man himself. He was looking over at me with a mouth half full of sandwich, the rest of which he held in his hands. It seemed I had arrived during lunch.

He was a stocky sort, dressed in that universal dark-blue mechanic's outfit underneath a stained yellow hat with his business name on it. A patch over the heart read "Arnold," I could see, as it halfway jutted out from under the coat he was wearing. It was warmer in that office, but not by much, I was depressed to find out. What little heat there was came from a small space heater set near to his desk.

Rising from his chair, he wiped his thick hands on his thighs and started to come around the desk. "I was just having some lunch."

"I see that," I responded.

He extended a hand toward me, and after a half second of hesitation I shook it. I could see some sort of tattoo on his wrist poking out from his sleeve, so old that the edges had begun to blur. "Arnold Brandt. So, what can I do ya for?"

The man's brown eyes were friendly enough. He certainly didn't look a bad sort, so I decided to be a bit more direct than I initially thought. "Well, I reckon I need to talk to you about a car."

He leaned back, catching a seat on the corner of the desk. Arms crossed, he nodded. "To buy? Or to fix? I have gotten mostly out of the car selling business, I'll warn you, but I still have a few left."

I shook my head and chuckled. "I don't reckon this car is fixable at this point. No, I need to talk to you about your purple car."

He stiffened a bit but tried to mask it, I could tell. "I don't have a purple car. Not anymore."

"You are correct," I winked. "Seems it was causing a bit of fuss, so I took care of it."

His eyes narrowed. "What did you say your name was?"

"I didn't. But it's Howard Marsh."

I caught a glimpse of wide eyes as he bolted past me. He was quicker than he looked, those stocky legs bulling him past me and out the door. He'd tried to catch me with a stiff arm, but I managed to step out of the way rather than be shoved back into the wall. As it was, I almost tripped over myself, so it was a couple seconds before I could start my pursuit. "Fuck me," I muttered under my breath, heading for the door.

The door had not yet shut, so slamming it wide enough for me to fit through, I raced after the man. He was already a good distance ahead of me, I was dismayed to see. Legs pounding, the two of us raced down the hill toward the junkyard. "Brandt! I just want to talk, damn it!" I could see him flinch a bit when I yelled, so I know he heard me. However, he did not slow.

By the time he reached the fence I was damn near wheezing. He had managed to put a little more distance between us as well, such that he was able to slam the gate shut and snap the lock. I could see through the fence that as soon as he got it locked, he just carried on running.

I stopped, hands on knees, wanting to throw up. "Goddamn it, man, stop!" I managed to get out.

And then he was gone, having disappeared into the maze of junk cars.

Cussing a blue streak, I walked over to the lock. I gave it a tug, just in case he hadn't managed to click it all the way closed. I, of course, had no such luck. So with a few muttered words and a twiddle of the fingers, I tapped it.

Instead of falling open it pulsed red and gave my hand a shock, enough to send my already rather errant hair standing on end. Sucking my fingertip to try and ease the pain, I stepped back. I summoned up my little magic-sniffing orb again. Sure enough the lock was bespelled, a fat little sigil precisely drawn on its surface.

This fucking nobody was better at glyphs than me—by a fucking long shot! Not gonna lie, that pissed me off. Should that anger have been directed a bit more inwards? Perhaps. But it would have had to fight for space in my burning lungs, and there was not to spare just then, so fuck Brandt.

I sent the orb around my surroundings while I contemplated how to go about this. I could just leave, maybe send HD or someone to talk to Brandt. But I was guessing that if my name set him off like that, likely any of the Marsh clan would set him off. I'd hate for this guy to spring a trap on my kin now that he knew we were wise to him.

The orb turned up a fat lot of nothing other than that lock. I thought of just blasting it away, but I worried that

I should maybe conserve as much of my juice as possible. So with a grunt, I jumped up and effortlessly pulled myself over the fence with my usual effortless grace.

Rather, I *would* have, had my coat not caught on the top of the fence. Instead of landing full of grace and vigor, my coat snagged, causing me to fall into the fence. My arms were pulled up, just about dislocating my arms from my shoulders as the coat pulled over my head. Then with a loud rip it, the metal tore through and I fell to the ground with a dull thud.

I lay there groaning for a moment, wondering if my arms were still attached. The only real indication that they were was on account of how much they hurt. On top of that, all the wind had been knocked out of me, as if I hadn't already been out of breath bad enough. I was fairly certain I would just lay there a bit and regret all of my life choices, maybe consider just dying altogether to put myself out of my misery for good. But before the pity party could even properly begin, the dulcet tones of HD's voice reached my ears.

"Howard, are you ok? What the fuck is going on?"

I had hoped he had been too busy looking in a book or something to notice my chase down the hill. I saw now that that was not the case. Rather, I heard it, as my eyes were still held tight shut against the pain and indignity.

I refused to look at him. If I did, I would probably leave. "Yes. No. Go back to the car."

"Son, you're fucking hurt—I'm not going back to the fucking car!"

I did not want to talk; I wanted to die and end my suffering. So, my life being what it is, I instead staggered to my feet and faced him. "Look. I'm fine. Now go away. Thank you. Go away."

He was doing that thing where his face got all scrunched up with thought, which usually was a good thing, but in this moment I could have gleefully backed over him with a car. "Just get out of there, then. Come back to the car and quit being dumb."

"Uncle. Go. Please." My shoulders felt like they were on fire, but the pain was beginning to dull to a low roar. It matched the lingering pain in my chin, which was still smarting from yesterday. This made it difficult, but I had used my most sincere grown-up voice. There was no telling what all wards and sigils he might have dotted the area with. I mean, he ran in here for a reason.

"How about I wait here, then? Compromise."

It got a little heated, and there may have been a few curses lobbed through the fence. But in the end he listened to me, I listened to him, and we came to the compromise I could live with, even if it made him all sorts of grumpy. That, I could deal with later.

I had bigger fish to fry.

Oo, Baby, It's a Wild World

Behind me HD was walking back up the hill a little ways, which is where we'd finally settled on. In front of me was a maze of cars. Most were only one high, but in some places Arnold had piled crushed cars into stacks three or four. It had the effect of obscuring my vision pretty well at times, while at others I could see for a good forty feet or so. And while I had seen down which row my quarry had run, I could see that it quickly twisted away and out of sight.

Squaring my sore shoulders, I set off toward where I had last seen the man. My orb, I set to roving back and forth in front of me in a lazy figure eight. I had to walk real slow to give it time to cover both sides, in case he had laid some sort of trap.

The wind began to blow a bit, and it was painfully cold. The tear in my jacket let it right in and it curled around my ribs like icy little fingers. Pulling my coat tighter just made the tear wider, I found, so I resigned myself to being cold. Because why not, right? It was just going to be a shit day all 'round.

My annoyance at Brandt had transitioned to just being pissed off. The energy flowing through me started to take on an angry tone, like it was gnashing at the teeth to be used. I knew I would have to be careful; whenever I got like this, sometimes things had a way of getting away from me. Though if my mood got much worse, I might've just let it.

My orb started spotting the occasional glyph on the trunks of some of the cars. I recognized the sigil as the same from the padlock on the gate though, so I just left them be, though I admit I was mighty curious as to just what he had tucked away inside them junk cars. I mean, I had been known on occasion perhaps to . . . *liberate* . . . goods that didn't entirely belong to me at the point I acquired them. But just as heavy of a factor is I was sometimes just fucking curious. I like knowing what's inside that box, or behind that gate, or in that old house. I could get plum ate up with it, till I had to satisfy it or go mad.

I could feel that building up the more I thought about those locked trunks.

But then I remembered my initial worry that the purple car had a body in the trunk, and that feeling began to fade. Maybe old Brandt was some sort of serial killer? What the fuck had I stumbled in to . . .

I came to a fork in the row and took a left. One way was as good as another, I figured; eventually I would find him. Though, knowing my luck, he had taken a right, and this was the long way around. Or it led to a dead end and I would have to backtrack.

My tiny glowing buddy found a pair of small sigils, these having been laid on a hubcap which was leaned up against the back tire of some old Chevy truck. They were different from the lock, but naturally I had no clue what they meant. I promised myself that when I got done with all this crap I would sit down with HD and learn a touch. Of course, I had made that promise a couple times before, but maybe twentieth time's the charm.

I stared at that hubcap longer than anyone had likely ever eyed a rusted hubcap off an old Chevy. I thought about poking it with a stick, but there wasn't one handy. In the end I decided to conjure up a little illusion. I stepped back and reached down into myself. That anger was still pretty strong in me, so it came bounding up from deep inside, begging to be used. I reigned it in, letting a trickle of Power thread its way down my arms. I made the proper gestures, and then I was looking at a fairly passable representation of myself.

I looked like shit, I thought. There was potential there, for sure, but hard living had taken its toll. When had my face got so gaunt looking?

It left me a little shaken, to be honest. I, as a rule, avoided mirrors for just this reason. No one likes to see their good looks fade and crumble under the weight of the world. After staring a moment longer, I gave my head a little shake and set the thing to walking.

It took two steps and then things popped off.

That hubcap flew right through my illusion. It whipped up so fast I was pretty sure had that been the actual me, and not an image, I would be short a head right now. It hurtled right through imaginary me, causing the image to dissipate, and slammed into a stack of crushed cars twenty feet away.

That's when this wailing sound started up by where the hubcap landed, and dogs began to bark.

They did not sound like happy dogs.

Good Puppy

I like dogs alright, but these dogs were clearly in protection mode. They were also getting closer with a quickness. I heard at least three of them headed my way, so my first move was to climb up on top of the car closest to me. I could have run, but I didn't really want to risk running up on another of those trap sigils.

This was not my first rodeo with dogs by any stretch. If you do as much trespassing and light theft as I have, you will have the odd run in or two. Needless to say, I could handle them, though I wasn't wild about having to spend more of my Power. Who knows what all else could be ahead of me? I cursed myself for leaving Horace behind like an idiot. There was nothing to be done, however.

I sat there on the battered hood of that old car and marshalled my Power. Thankfully that siren stopped, letting me focus a bit better. The dogs would be there any second, from the sounds of things, so digging in my pocket, I pulled out my key ring. I only had the one key to my shed padlock, but it jangled with a number of other implements I occasionally found useful. I fingered through them till I found the one I was looking for: a small whistle.

Its metal was warm against my lips, having been safely ensconced inside my pocket up against my thighs, which felt like they might be the only part of me that wasn't icy cold. Quietly I sang a few words into the whistle. It began to hum, resonating with my voice, occasionally with the faintest whisper of a trilling noise as my breath blew inside it. The metal grew warmer the longer I sang till it was almost too hot to hold onto.

Three large mutts came racing around the corner then. They were big dogs, but fat. These were not lethal junkyard dogs; these were yard dogs playing at being fierce. Not to say they like as not wouldn't bite the mess out of me, but if I tried hard enough, I might could have just scared them off.

Instead, I blew the whistle. It was hot against my lips, like a bit of fresh coffee. It was hard to keep them there, but the more I blew, the cooler they got, thankfully.

Instead of your usual whistle noises, out came a flow of pale purple light. It beelined straight for each of them dogs, striking them right in the forehead. In a heartbeat their dispositions changed, totally flipping a one-eighty.

Now instead of racing toward me, they were bounding like puppies. The barking stopped and their tails began wagging about, bit to bust.

So I climbed off that car and let them jump on me for a second. I rubbed them all, scratching behind their ears and such, calling them good boys. They ate it right up. You'd have thought I raised them from puppies or had a pocket slap full of Milk-Bones.

My grandfather had only taught me a few spells before he passed, precious few. But of them, this one was by far my favorite. I just wished it worked on humans. Would've made my life a shit load easier.

It took a few seconds, but I got them calmed down. Once they had, I took stock. I had a good bit of Power left, but things had clearly escalated. The man had, for all intents, tried to kill me. I was not gonna go into a situation like that with "a good bit."

I wanted a fuckton.

So I pulled a little baggy out of my pocket and retrieved a trio of pills. Careful not to drop them, I set them where, a moment ago, I had been sitting. Taking out my keys again, I selected a piece of metal I kept on it for just these occasions. Carefully, I ground up the pills, making sure to keep my body between them and the wind. Bits of rust found their way into the mix, turning the powder a reddish brown instead of its usual white.

I didn't much mind. It all goes up the nose the same way.

A moment later I was wiping my nose. The pills hit my body quick, and I swear I felt my eyes dilating. Breathing in deep, I wet my finger and used it to get up the remains my nose had missed, rubbing it on my gums. By the time it was all clean, I was ready. I was so twitchy with my newfound high I felt like I could pop. I only had to wipe away a little nudge of blood from my nose, which I knew was a sure sign I was only one crash away from reeeeeally regretting having done this. I just had to hope it didn't come until after I handled Brandt.

I looked at the dogs. "Let's do this."

Moving Apace

I sent away my little orb and instead called back up my illusion. I set it out in front of me, moving at a pretty good clip, and followed along behind by about a good twenty paces. Them pups just hung around my legs, getting a bit underfoot at times, but I preferred that than to have them chasing along after me looking to take a chunk out of my ass.

I was taking a gamble that any other traps the man had set up would be similar to that first one, but in truth I was so hopped up I wasn't much in the way of caring. I just wanted through with this. So I struck up a jog and sped up my illusion to match.

All the rows looked about the same to me, just stacks and jumbles of cars to either side. Like as not all full of creepy crawlies just waiting to sting or bite you, I imagined, suddenly thankful it wasn't summertime and warm enough for such critters to thrive. Wasps are an especial hatred of mine.

Two more times, hubcaps "killed" my illusion and alarms went off. I just summoned it back up and carried on. I imagined that wherever Brandt was hiding, he was probably pissing himself at the fact his traps weren't working. It made me feel all warm and fuzzy inside.

I could see the tractor trailers a little better now and set myself toward working in their direction. I figured if the man was headed someplace, it was like as not there. The path I was on, though, didn't seem to be going in quite that direction.

So I said screw it and started climbing over cars. I hopped up on the trunk of one car, then jumped to the next, then over onto a third, which had me set up in a new set of rows. Behind me the dogs took to whining as I left them behind, but I couldn't be bothered with that. I debated trying out this new pathway but then just decided that a straight line by going over the rows of cars would likely be safer, and certainly quicker. So long as I didn't trip and fall between a couple, that is.

By the time I was adjacent to the row that separated me from the tractor trailers I had only managed to get one small cut. I had sliced my hand on bit of rusted tailgate, but I was so juiced from the drugs I didn't really feel it. I just noticed the blood, but having nothing to wrap it in, I just let it be.

I squatted on the hood of a Chrysler and eyed the clearing in front of me, holding my hand to the side so that the blood wouldn't drip on my pants. It looked to me to be the heart of Brandt's operation. There were those two big tractor trailers sitting on rotted-out tires. The trucking company logos on the sides had long faded away, so clearly they had been there some time. They were set side by side, so close you couldn't have fit my bleeding hand between them.

There was also a small tin shed next to a mountain of tires, most of which were blown with the wire showing. Set next to that was some sort of metal box with an open front. A few wires ran from it, so I guess it had power for something, but I couldn't tell what it was. It was big enough inside that I might not could have touched its ceiling and was easily three times as long. It was quite the mystery.

I did not see Brandt. But If I had to guess, the clunking noise coming from inside that shed would be coming from him. I weighed my options. I wanted to kill the man, but that would lead to a number of questions that no cop would believe the answers to, even if I had been the killing type. No, I couldn't kill him without going to jail, and if I was being really honest with myself, I didn't have the stomach for killing.

I just needed to talk to the damn fool—without getting killed in the process. Talk to him, and convince him to go see Granny and ask forgiveness. Which, being something I had done in the past to poor result, I did not envy him for.

If this was the man's base of operations, I guessed it would probably be the most warded and bespelled place so far. I really should have just taken my time and slowly eased my way into the place, but I was far too twitchy for that. Instead I just sent my illusion out in front once again and started heading for the shed.

No hubcaps tried to kill me, but that damn siren sure went off again. Damn thing sounded like a demon cat or something, just screeching away. Knowing the game was up now and any thought of a stealthy approach was gone, I yelled out, "Brandt, I just want to talk, is all! I surprised you, you tried to kill me, let's call it even!"

The clanging stopped for a second, and I was pretty sure I heard a muffled "fuck" come from inside the shed. I stopped where I was, not wanting to get too close. For all I knew he had a gun tucked away in there ready to pop one in me. I could handle guns in a pinch, but I would need a bit of time. I was suddenly thankful that shed didn't have a window from which he could shoot out of.

My only warning was the faint pulse of magic being used nearby.

And then the wall of the shed exploded outwards toward me.

More Than Meets the Eye

A bit of wood struck my knee hard enough to stagger me. I was lucky it struck sideways or it might have gone right through. As it was, I cried out in pain as I reeled backwards and landed on my ass. It wasn't broke, but it sure as hell was in a lot of pain. I couldn't fully focus on that, however, as much as I would have liked to. Instead, the bulk of my attention was drawn to the monstrosity that had burst out of the shed.

It was a good ten feet tall, with the same general outline of a human: two arms, two legs, and a head. But beyond that, all similarities to anything living ended. Instead, this . . . *thing* had been built of car parts. Its chest was broad, made of a car hood. Its legs looked like bundles of exhaust pipes that had been welded together, same for its arms. Its head was a small engine with a pair of headlights mounted on the front. They were glowing with an eerie green light even though it was clear they were not actually connected to anything.

Its hands, though, drew most of my interest-they ended in jagged slivers of sharpened metal. If I had to guess, they had started life as lawnmower blades before being turned into Marsh slicers. Each was a good foot in length, and altogether there were seven of them.

It's weird how the mind works. In that moment what bothered me most was not my impending death, but the lack of symmetry—not six blades, not eight. The man had made it with *seven*. Who does that? A goddamn serial killer, that's who.

"Steering Golem! Kill!" came a shout from inside the shed.

The fool had made a fucking golem and named it for a pun. Looking up, I could see where he had put the Word of Life on what would be its forehead. Instead of paint, the ass had welded it in place. I was boned.

I scrambled to my feet. The only thing I had going for me is that I was marginally faster, even though I was limping quite badly. It was heading for me with steps that were scary loud and sent up puffs of dirt and dust. I, meanwhile, didn't know what in the hell to do.

To buy me some time, I reached down deep and pulled out a real strong force. Launching from my hands a wave of purple energy, it slammed into the thing, staggering it for a moment and forcing it back a couple of steps. I used the time I found to pull out my pill baggy and swallow the lot of them. They would hit in a minute, and then I would either use up a lot of energy quick or burn out and die, my brain oozing out the side of my head.

The problem was I didn't have anything that could really handle metal. And killing Arnold, which had reached new levels in my list of life goals, would not stop the damn thing. It would then just be operating without a master, and who knew what it might do once it had finished carrying out its final orders to mush me into pulp.

It was coming toward me again, Brandt hopping up and down like an excited little monkey in the background. He was whooping and yelling, all excited, acting like a damn cheerleader as this thing set off to kill me. Had he not had a multiton monster between me and him I would have smacked him right across his stupid fucking face.

I was hobbling away as quickly as I could, but it was shaping up to be a losing battle for the moment. I looked frantically around for any sort of anything I could use to try and beat the damn thing. My eyes looked over to that weird box. Inching closer, I could read the faded letters on it: Overbuilt Car Crusher.

I looked from the beast to the crusher. If I could get it inside there . . .

Before I could make a move, I noticed barking. The dogs seemed to have found me once again. I glanced to my right, and sure enough they were racing toward me as fast as their legs would take them. And then they became aware of the fact I was under threat.

I frantically grabbed at my pocket, trying to get the whistle out. But the dogs saw their new friend was in danger and leapt to the attack. I don't know who screamed louder, me or Brandt. It didn't matter, though.

I caught a face full of blood as the golem destroyed those poor dogs. It was hot on my face, the only real warmth I had felt since stepping out of the car. And then the golem wasn't the only thing seeing red.

The drugs were taking effect and I pulled on them, hard. I could feel the damage they were doing to my innards, but it was do or die time, and I was no longer thinking my most clearly. I was a ball of unspent energy and rage, and both were about to pour out of me like a waterfall.

Three words left my mouth, and I leapt. My legs felt like coiled springs, even with my wounded knee. I knew I would pay for it later, but at that moment I was able to ignore it. I jumped through the cold air and it ripped through my coat, making a fluttering sound. I didn't care—I was beyond caring. Revenge would be mine, and that was all that mattered.

I clamored up on top of the car crusher. Brandt was standing a dozen feet away, looking up at me with his jaw dropped open. It looked like he was on the verge of tears, I supposed over the death of his dogs. I scowled at him.

"Fuck you, Brandt." I extended a hand and voiced words of Power. Pure force struck him. Instead of knocking him back, though, a bit of a glow emanated from beneath his shirt. It pulsed blue. I glared venomously and twisted my hand, repeating the word.

There was a cracking sound, and Brandt was thrown back into the shed. As he flew, his chest erupted in blue-black fireworks as his protective amulet was overloaded by my spell. He struck the wall, but at the last moment I eased up on the force and used it to fractionally cushion his fall. I wanted him out of the game, not dead.

Well, no, I *did* want him dead. Just not as bad as I wanted to stay out of prison.

The monster had lumbered much closer. It swung one of its powerful arms at me and I jumped back. Its massive claws whooshed through the air so close to me that I could feel the wind of them passing. One even snagged my coat. Had it not been so sharp that it just sliced right through, it would likely have snatched me hard to the right.

My knee threatened to buckle under me at any moment, but I pushed it harder. The drugs were filling my blood and I felt like I was on fire. My skin tingled and I was sure my hair was standing straight up. One word had my legs filling with power, more than I think I'd ever pumped into them before, and then I used my magic-pumped legs to push beneath me.

I powered up into the air a dozen feet above the thing. As I flew up, it reached for me and struck my foot with one of its claws. Luckily it was the flat of the blade, though it did manage to cut a gash on my calf as I soared past. I screamed, as I was pretty sure my ankle was broken.

The blow spun me around, but thankfully that is what I needed anyway; it was the one small blessing in this whole encounter. I was behind the thing now, and I got ready to land on legs that, though stout with Power, were very likely broken to some degree or other. It was going to be bad, and that was before I saw that the damn thing was already starting to wheel on me.

I hit the ground, and I instantly buckled into a heap. I had only *thought* I wanted to die earlier, I realized. When weight hit my ankle I screamed, and I thought I was going to black out. But digging deep, I turned that scream into a shouted word as I pulled Power and slammed it into the golem. It staggered back, fighting against my force. I poured everything I had into it, inching the damned thing until it was fully inside the car crusher. I could tell my nose was bleeding, mixing with the dog blood that covered my face. I knew my ears would be next, and then I would black out. I had to end this.

With one final, massive push I slammed the thing into the back of the box. I felt my ears pop, and the golem hit with a deafening clang that actually rocked the whole shebang back a fraction. Its red eyes seemed to glare at me—at least that's how it felt. I just smiled back.

I scraped up the last of my Power to hold it in place while I hobbled over to the controls. I lifted the lever that read CRUSH, and then collapsed to the ground. I landed on my broken ankle, and I felt bone grind on bone. It was all I could do to not pass out. Control of my spell left me for a moment, though, and I heard it coming toward me once more.

The tank was empty; all I had left were fumes and likely a couple of ulcers. I was flickering between lucidity and unconsciousness, but in one last flash of light I took those fumes and shoved.

And then it turned black.

That Guy

I came to sometime later. I wasn't sure how long it had been; all I really knew was that someone was shaking me back to life. Opening my eyes I saw HD hunched over me, tears flowing freely down his face. When he saw my eyes open, he cut loose this squawk and took me up in a hug so tight I thought I might not ever see daylight again.

"Goddamn, boy, you had me so scared! Never fucking do that again, you hear me? Or I promise I will kick your ass!"

I mumbled something into his chest. I don't even know what. I wasn't thinking very clearly.

He turned me loose a bit and gently lowered me back down. "You!" he yelled, pointing. "Get over here!"

I turned my head to look at where he was pointing. A very sheepish-looking, clearly crying Brandt was standing there. The man slowly walked over. "Mr. Marsh . . . your uncle here sorta spelled things out a bit. I'm sorry. I'd just heard so much about all . . . all you Marshes, I thought you'd come to kill me." He paused and swallowed. "I really am sorry. You'll tell your Granny that, right?"

"Nope," I grinned. Well, I hoped it was a grin. In truth I was mostly just trying to not vomit. But I tried to put on my most wicked aura. "You can tell her yourself. And my daddy."

He paled, clearly shaken. "Which . . . which one is your daddy?"

This time I knew I nailed the grin. "Jack."

He groaned.

And then I faded out again. I felt a little better this time, though.

It feels good to share the misery sometimes.

Preaching to the Choir

I t is a special sort of hell to be so cold that you're shivering and have a broken ankle, even if it is in a cast.

My string of great luck was running well apace, as last night, right about midnight, my space heater broke. I'd thrown on every blanket and such that I owned, and I might have been alright if I hadn't had to open my door to go take a piss. Hobbling on a crutch like I was meant I was slow-moving, and what little heat I had built up disappeared into the frosty morning.

So now I was sitting under the blankets trying to self-medicate. The doctor I'd seen had been new, and he'd given me the good stuff for pain. But with a history like mine, well, I was supplementing. Which meant that if I could tough it out a bit longer, pain wouldn't be an issue for a few hours.

Of course there was, as always, a chance that the pain wouldn't be an issue for, well, ever. But that was the cost of being me, I reckoned, and I risked it.

I was pretty well fucked. The whole Brandt debacle had netted me absolutely no money, and in fact I now had some medical bills I wasn't going to pay on top of that. And with a broken ankle, all my usual methods of earning money were pretty much out. Coupled with my self-medication, I was going to be flat out of drugs soon too. But that was tomorrow's problem. And the day after, Anna would be back around to make my life a little better.

I just had to make it till then. It couldn't get much worse, I reckoned, so I settled in to have a righteous pity party until the high kicked in proper.

Three massive booms against the metal of my shed door came on so loud that I actually screamed a little. Which, I reckon, gave whoever was knocking on my door a heads up that I was home, so with a rattling jumble of sound up it flew, letting in the mid afternoon sun, blinding me.

"Fuck," I shouted, raising up my hand to shield my eyes. I didn't even try to get up, or run; that ship had sailed. I could see a massive form standing in my open doorway, and inside I cursed myself for thinking it couldn't get worse. I knew better.

"Marsh," came the deep voice of Preach. There was some real anger there, and I knew that didn't bode well for me.

He stepped into my shed and walked up beside my couch where I lay cocooned.

"Preach." I tried to play it cool, though the rather feminine shriek I had let out seconds before probably didn't help my case much.

"Did you do it?"

I could have lied. I mean, arguably it's what I do best. But it's mighty hard to lie to someone with Power, as my Granny has bludgeoned into my head over, and over, and over, always to my detriment. I didn't know why—if it was a spell, or just some sort of innate thing that having a lot of Power would get you—but I knew I hadn't ever had much luck lying to anyone more magically powerful than me.

"Yeah."

Preach loosed a long, slow breath. Clearly he was trying to keep from smacking sheer hell out of me.

"Granny order it?"

I would have loved to pin it on the old bitch, but when she found out I did because Preach went knocking on her door, I would be well and truly fucked then. "No. But it was the right thing to do. And I reckon when you think it through, you'll know I'm right. Ain't nothing like the Hog of the Road gonna let something like that work without it going to his advantage. What, you were gonna put holy water in the barbeque sauce?"

He flinched a little, just enough for me to know I struck some sort of nerve. But that passed mighty quick, and all that was left was the anger. He spoke slow, making each word real clear. "You're blessed that I am a man of God and His teachings."

Then, of course, my smart mouth showed up. " 'Turn the other cheek' teaching, or 'summon up the bears to eat the kids' teachings?"

I thought he was gonna hit me. "Keep on, and I'll leave you wishing for bears, son."

I decided to shut up.

"Your uncle told me a bit of what you went through, and that's the only thing saving you right now. You did a good thing with that tow trucker, but in a dumb way, and I have to suffer for it."

"I mean—"

He cut me off with a look. "You're going to find some way to make this right."

It wasn't a question, and it was said with some bone-chilling intensity. He turned and stalked from my shed, at the last second turning his head to look over his shoulder at me. "I'll be praying for you."

Goddamn if that didn't sound like a threat.

He left without bothering to close my door, letting cold wind blow in. I knew I needed to get up and shut it, but honestly I was kinda thinking freezing to death could be a blessing at this point.

Through the open door waddled Horace. My possum pal trundled up onto my couch with me, somehow missing my cast, and curled up onto my chest. He didn't purr—he wasn't no cat—but he did look up at me with those big softie eyes of his, and I melted a little. He grunted as I scritched him behind the ears like he liked, and I started to feel his warmth flow onto me.

Life was shit. But maybe it was a little less shit just at that moment.

THE BRIAR WITCH

Being the Sixth Tale in the Redemption of Howard Marsh.

Prologue

Kandra had not yet gotten used to the unending humidity of the late Alabama summer. It wrapped around her like a cloak, leaving her dripping with sweat. She knew she wasn't dressed right for a traipse through a swamp, but then gutterpunks don't have a lot of clothes as a rule. If she was going to stay here, and she was beginning to think she might, she was going to have to invest in clothes suited to the weather.

She was not a woodsy kind of girl. But the longer she spent in Jubal County, the more she found herself wanting to become one. Four years spent on the road, hopping trains and thumbing rides from big city to big city had left her feeling . . . empty. And this cypress swamp was filling her back up.

Slapping her neck, she pulled back her hand and saw it was smeared with blood. She wiped it on the hem of her tattered black shirt. "Being *in* nature might be filling me back up, but nature itself is clearly trying to drain it back out of me," she said out loud, instantly feeling weird for having done so. She was glad none of the others were around in that moment.

Her boots were coated in mud, splatters of the brown goo having made their way up past her knees in a few places. Her heavily patched black jeans were likely ruined, and she was surprised to find she didn't care. Emily, one of the wives back at the camp, had offered to let her borrow some clothes. Kandra knew she should have taken her up on her offered kindness, but the last shreds of her old life were in what she wore, and to toss them to the side . . . she just wasn't quite ready to fully make that plunge.

The day was coming, though—she could feel it as clearly as she could feel the sun's warmth beating down onto her face through the cypress limbs. The soft ground made faint sucking sounds as she wandered along, water fairly quickly filling her tracks as she went. Other than the sounds she made, the only noise came from the humming drone of the myriad of bugs out there and the occasional cry of some bird. She thought it might be that sense of silence that she most loved. Her life before had been one of the steady rumble of car engines as they passed her by on the interstate, or the clacking of trains on their tracks. The comparison . . .

She laughed out loud. There was no comparison.

The trees were thicker here, giving her some much welcome shade. She guessed she had walked a good four miles from the camp, maybe even a little farther. It was the farthest she had roamed so far, but Johnny had assured her that except for snakes there was nothing to really worry about. She still caught herself thinking about alligators, but they'd all insisted to her there were none in the county.

A low rumble in her stomach reminded her how it was getting close to lunchtime. She had packed a few protein bars, but she didn't want to stop and go digging through her pack just yet. The little trail she was on, which she guessed had been made by deer, was threading toward a fairly dark-looking thicket up ahead. Tucking an errant dread behind her ear, she made for it in hopes it would have ground firm enough to have lunch on.

A curse escaped her as a briar tore at her shirt, tearing another hole in it and raising a thin line of blood across her pale skin. Looking ahead she could see that thicket was just that: a maze of briars. She sighed, her hopes dashed. Or, she thought, looking down at her shirt, torn to shreds.

There was a hint of something darker in the midst of the brush, but her eyes could not fully make out what it might be. It looked as though it could be the corner of a house, or maybe a jumble of logs. Her curiosity was piqued, but the thought of fighting with all those briars reigned it under control.

The air suddenly felt thicker, and a faint smell, like something spoiled, came up to fill her nostrils. Clearly there was something dead up ahead, which further put a damper on her explorations. So though that little shack or whatever was interesting, it wasn't worth breathing in that stench to do so.

With a shrug she turned back down the little path. There had been a large log a mile back, if she didn't find some other stump or the like to sit on before then. Muddy jeans were not a problem, but she would be damned if she was going to be traipsing around with a wet ass from sitting on the ground.

Something darted on the edge of her vision. She turned but didn't see anything. Craning her head, she tried to spot whatever bird or deer she had spooked, but there was nothing. All she could see was the little trail and the thick brush.

To one side, a limb snapped. Her head darted in that direction, but still she saw nothing. There was something there now—she was sure of it. She was suddenly very aware of exactly how alone she was out there.

"Hello?" she called out. There was no answer.

She stood there, stock still for a couple of minutes. The only sound was the pounding of her heart, and very distantly, some sort of bird. She began to calm, and her heart slowed. Whatever it had been, it was gone now.

It reminded her of her first day out there, when an armadillo had come scuttling up out of the brush. It was small but had made such a racket she was sure that something huge had been tearing along through the bushes. She smiled at the thought, laughing at herself a bit, breaking the last of that panicked feeling loose from her chest.

From nowhere, Kandra was sent flying forward by something slamming into her back. Her face collided head-on with a tree and she felt her nose break, her piercing tearing free on a chunk of bark. She spat as she landed, a cough of blood and teeth fountaining from what was likely a broken jaw as well. Through the torrent of pain she could hear the snarl of some animal leaping for her.

She tried scrambling away, blood gushing from her ruined face. She turned just in time to see the inky black beast clamp down on her throat.

SUNDAY BEST, SUNDAY REST

I woke up on the floor, my cheek in a puddle of my own drool. I had perhaps taken one too many downers, I decided, then realized the fact I woke up at all meant that could not be the case. I had simply taken *almost* one too many downers.

It was full dark in my shed, which was a little off. Usually when I crashed like that, I left a light on, or left the door open. It was mildly disconcerting, so I just lay there and tried to go back to sleep. The concrete was too unforgiving, though, so after a good ten minutes of trying I gave up. My cheek was sticky with what I hoped was my own slobber.

With a groan I staggered to my feet. I wobbled a bit, but after a few seconds I steadied myself and made my way to the shed door. With a grunt I rolled it up, immediately regretting every moment of my life that had led to this point. Sunlight poured in, blinding me. I stepped back, trying to cover my eyes, and tripped over something. I landed on my ass with a thud, rattling my half-blind eyes in their sockets.

I let loose a string of curses so foul they could have peeled paint off a wall.

"Mornin' to you too, Marsh," came a calm, smooth voice. I knew that voice, and knew it well, but was in no mind at that moment to figure it out.

"I'm sunblinded, so if you're gonna kill me, do it quick and get me out my misery."

I heard the laughter of a half dozen people flow, that of both men and women. "I reckon we'll let you live this time," came that same voice.

I shielded my eyes and rose to my feet once again. My eyes were coming around, though they hated every second of it. Everyone was shadows for a second, and then they began to come into focus.

"Ah, mornin', Johnny," I said, recognizing the man at last. I nodded to the woman at his side. "Emily."

Johnny was a tall man, well over six feet, and born with looks that would have made a New York model jealous. He was funny, and kind, and super talented. Normally that was a surefire recipe for me to take a disliking to someone, but with him . . . hell, everyone loved Johnny.

He was the best fiddle player in Jubal County—which is maybe not the claim to fame in this century that it would have been in the last, but still. He was good enough that even the uptight religious types forgave him his hippie lifestyle out at the Camp, so long as he played all the church socials.

His wife, Emily, was at his side, her arms full of clothes, and behind them were the other men and women of the Camp, in various stages of undress. They looked to be stripping down outta their everyday clothes, which was your standard hippie fare. Lots of flowy dresses and shit.

"Must be playing today," I said.

Johnny grinned and gave a little half bow. "Playing the Thomas wedding over in Sumpville, at the Methodist church. Good day for it, too. They're lucky to be missing all this bad weather we've been having."

Johnny and his group of merry reprobates were a band, playing pretty much whatever you needed them to. Seeing as the Camp, which they called home, was in the middle of a swamp, they kept their show clothes, and most of their gear, in the shed next to mine.

I fumbled in my pocket for a smoke, wishing the sun would dim a bit all the while. "I suppose so. I ain't much of one for weddings."

"One day, Marsh, I will play you a show like no other at your wedding. I can feel it." The man smiled at me, and with a sinking feeling I suspected he was right. Johnny didn't know it, but he had more than a bit of Power to him, I suspected. It's partly what made his fiddle playing so irresistible.

I just grunted. I needed coffee blacker than midnight and twice as strong, or some assorted goodies out of my fun box, before I would be much good for conversatin'.

Emily was handing out dress shirts and ties to the other men. She was already dressed in her Sunday best, I saw, moving with all the grace of a ballet dancer, sunlight causing her blonde hair to shine gold. It was quite a sight, I had to admit. Some couples, man . . .

"Howard, do you think you could help us with something?" Emily was one of the few that called me Howard. Most folks, I would have begrudged them that. But not her. "One of our new friends, she's taken to exploring the land around the Camp. She didn't come home last night, though. It's got me a little worried. Think you and maybe HD could give a little look for her?"

"We'd be looking—hell we looked a bit last night, but we couldn't cancel on this wedding. Kandra is a bit of a city girl, but she's taken to our ways with an easy grace." A little bit of worry was on Johnny's face, but it was mixed with a soft pride as he spoke. "She probably wandered a bit farther than normal and got lost. She's been staying gone longer each time, and she told us she might overnight it . . . but still. We worry."

Inwardly I groaned. The last thing I wanted to do was go wandering through a swamp looking for one of the Camp's strays. If I hadn't been thinking of getting up with HD today anyway I would have tried to weasel out of it. I'd have failed, 'cause when angels come to earth like Emily and Johnny ask you something, you do it, but I would have tried.

And honestly, I wasn't awake enough to try and fight about it. "Yeah, I reckon. I needed to see HD anyways."

Emily gave my cheek a quick peck. "You're a doll as always, Howard."

Johnny was buttoning up his shirt. "When y'all find her, hang around the Camp till we get back. We'll have a little to-do, drink some of your daddy's 'shine. We left a big stew slow cooking, so there will be plenty to eat. Hell, you know how we do."

I did indeed. A little traipse through the mud would suck, but a night out at the Camp always proved to be a bit magic. I had been to them more than a few times over the years.

"Ah, what the hell. Someone call up HD and get him over here. Sooner started, sooner done."

"Emily said we would be able to count on you!" Johnny smiled. "I'm glad you woke up when you did. Quite a bit of providence."

Truth be told, I was wanting to talk with HD so we could keep diving into this grimoire I took off Brandt a few months back. He was the uncle I got along best with, and he knew more about sigils and shit than anyone I knew. Even better, I could chat him up and he wouldn't just go back cryin' to Granny and rat me out first chance he got for trying to learn shit she probably didn't want me learning.

I set about getting ready to go—changing my shirt, pulling on cleanish socks, that sort of thing—just sorta biding my time. My ankle was healed up finally, but I was still going a little easy on it. Much as I could, at least. It had put me in a real bad place for a couple months, and I was only just now getting out of it. I'd put in a lot of really shitty hours in chicken houses just to keep me only two months behind on rent. And as my drug dealer knew better than to give me store credit, I had been dancing a real fine line there, too, to the point I was having some bad issues. If it hadn't been for Anna . . . I don't know. That might have been it for me.

Outside, the band was about ready. I needed them to go ahead and leave so I could get into my little box of oblivion. They were all cool with weed, but beyond that they got a little preachy. But then that was fucking everybody.

Emily called over, phone in her hand. "Hubert Dale said he would be over in about twenty minutes to pick you up."

My stomach growled a bit. "Tell him to get me a biscuit on the way, if you would," I shouted back.

A couple of minutes later the band was all loaded. Johnny loomed large in my doorway, giving me a final rundown of sorts. "Kandra is a white girl with dreads, dressed all punk style. You'll know her when you see her. Just tell her we sent you, and she should tag right along."

"Gotcha, boss," I said, wishing he would just go the fuck on so I could start my day off right finally.

He nodded, turning toward their van. "Thanks again, Marsh. See you this evening."

MARSHES IN MARSHES

By the time Uncle Hubert Dale rolled up in his old white van I was humming along fairly well. I had a cocktail of drugs flowing through my system, and as his tires rolled over the gravel I was rolling up a joint as a palate cleanser. As he came to a stop, the window lowered and a McDonald's biscuit sailed toward me.

I caught it deftly, the wrapper crinkling under my fingers. It was still warm, the heat of it flowing up into my fingers. "Sausage?" I asked.

"Bacon, egg, and cheese," replied my uncle as he climbed out of the van, a bag in hand.

"Fancy. What's the occasion?"

HD shrugged. He was not much taller than me, and almost as gaunt. His hair was a bit more than shoulder length, and every inch of it was an ashy gray. He wasn't that old, at least not old enough to be that gray, but he'd had a hard life.

He was the youngest of my four uncles, and far and away the one I was closest to. I was fond of uncle Rooster, too, but for the most part I didn't really have time for most of my family. They didn't have much time for me either, though, so it worked out nicely.

HD reached out and snagged the joint from my hand. Dropping the bag down beside me, he eased down onto the ground, leaning back against the frame of the rolling door. "Some hash browns in that bag if you want 'em," he said as he lit the joint. He held in a deep breath of the earthy smoke as I took a bite of my biscuit.

"Didn't take you long to get here," I said from around a mouthful.

He coughed out a cloud of smoke and held the joint back out to me. "I was already on the way over."

I chased my toke with another bite. He didn't offer up any reason as to why he had been bound for my little shed, and I just went with it. HD had a knack for knowing when he'd be needed. He couldn't really do much in the way of spell slinging, but his hunches were never wrong. Ever.

We sat in silence for a good ten minutes, enjoying that joint and the food. Wiping the crumbs from my shirt and tucking away the roach for later enjoyment, I climbed to my feet. I felt like I could run a mile at a full sprint. Not that I would, of course—my lungs would see to that—but boy, I was hyped.

"Uncle dearest, I ain't gonna lie, traipsing through a swamp ain't high on my list of fun activities. But the way I'm feeling . . . fuck it! Let's get to it!"

HD chuckled. "Glad to see you motivated for a change, boy. Let's ride this wave long as it lasts. Too early to hear too much bitching out of you."

The van bumped along the narrow dirt track that led to the Camp. More driveway than road, it had followed a ridgeline from where it split from Highway 17, easing down into the swampy bottomland that had been in Johnny's family for generations. I had always been oddly partial to swamps—not so much being in them, but seeing them from the road always gave me a bit of enjoyment. There was just something primal about them that I liked. They beat the hell out of a fucking pine forest, I'll tell you that much.

The drive led us through a large chunk of the marsh, at times more puddle and mud slick than anything that should have been driven on. HD's van would be more

brown than white by the time we were done here, I suspected, but then I wouldn't be the one who had to clean
it, so I didn't much care.

The trail took us up a slight rise to the highest point in
the swamp, though that was just a matter of a few feet
difference. The road firmed slightly, and as we made our
way slowly around a curve the Camp hovered into view.

The swamp flooded every few years, so the Camp had long
ago given up on any sort of permanent structure, giving
way to a mix of tent and hammock living. So instead of a
house, there was a large pavilion at the center of a copse
of old water oaks which acted as their communal space.
Around that were a riot of colors, as a hodgepodge of
old army tents, tented hammocks, and lean-tos dotted the
spaces on the small hill. Each had long ago been painted
over in a tumult of bright colors, made to resemble a field
of wild flowers as painted by a bunch of hippies who had
seen one too many Van Goghs.

As brimming with drugs as I was, such a riot of colors messed with my head. Painted flowers swirled and
swayed at the corner of my vision, twisting in a nonex-
istent breeze. For a brief second I caught a glimpse of
big cat eyes looking back at me from amongst the trees,
all aglow. Everything was flexing and pulsing, drumming
like a slow heartbeat. I could feel my eyes growing wider
and wider, trying to take it all in, and dryer as I fought the
urge to blink. We hit a bump in the road then, my eyes

closed for a split fucking second, and when they opened again everything had returned to normal. I cut loose a small sigh, already missing the weirdness.

We parked on the outskirts and made our way over to the pavilion. A pot of something that smelled amazing was slowly bubbling, and I was sorely tempted to try me a taste. I was making moves in that direction when HD, seeing the way my mind was working, called out. "Get on outta that!"

I huffed a bit, but in truth I wasn't really hungry, still full up on biscuit. It was more for show than anything. So I wandered over to where my uncle was standing, resisting my curiosity to go exploring the Camp whilst it was unattended. They were friends, so I wouldn't think of taking anything . . . but there were so many things to look at. And ok, maybe something might would have wandered into my pocket. But it was less likely here than most places.

Giving my head a little shake I turned back to HD. He was standing there with his eyes closed, head cocked to one side. His lips were moving, but no sound was coming out. A few moments later his eyes popped wide open and he pointed off to his right. "Couple miles that way," he said and started traipsing off in that direction.

We were a powerfully useful family if you were on our good side. Powerfully scary if not.

Outside his ability to know when he'd be needed, or expected, was the ability to locate people. I could find things, which is one way I earned some pocket change. But if you could get HD within a couple miles of a person, he could track 'em down. Which was useful, unless it was used on you as a kid while you was trying to hide from your granny.

There was a steady hum in the air, the constant drone of the millions of bugs that called the bottom of the marsh home. The air was thick, without any breeze to stir it, and we'd barely left the Camp before I felt sweat start to drip down my crack. A few steps later I had to slap the first biting fly off my arm, swearing as I did so.

One of, if not the most, annoying aspects of my uncle was the fact that the myriad of flying, biting things of South Alabama always seemed to avoid him like the plague. I was guaranteed to be ate up with bug bites by the time we walked out of here, but if he had a one, I would have been shocked. Waving away an ominous buzz from around my ear, I glared at HD. "I hate you."

He just smiled and winked at me. "I'm just impressed we made it this far before the bitchin' started up. Hell, I'm damn surprised we're even down here at all! Finding strays ain't exactly your bag." He paused, then laughed. "But then I bet Emily did the asking, didn't she?"

I snorted. "Ah, fuck off."

He chuckled, then his face grew serious. "So what's on your mind, boy? You're hopped up to the gills and can't hardly sit still but ain't said more than a dozen words to me. I know that brain of yours is churnin', so what's it on about?"

I thought for a second how to phrase things. I didn't want to be too leading, so as to see what HD could muster up on his own. "Just thinking about my general direction, I suppose."

HD shook his head slowly. "Young Howard, actually looking ahead! Who'd have thunk that day would come."

"Hush, you," I said. "Just . . . what with Krista teaching me about how to get a familiar, and now I got this book up offa Brandt, for the first time since I was, shit, like eight years old I feel like I'm really learning something. It feels pretty good, if I'm being honest. I just wish every other spell slinger in the county wasn't so scared of Granny sos I could go to them, get them to show me a bit more maybe."

HD pushed a branch up, ducking under it. "You are keeping this hush, right, boy? I sure as hell don't want to get on Momma's bad side. I love that you're learnin'—hell, you know I've been pushing that for years. But you got to be discreet."

"Trust me, I know. Granny made it real clear to me all them years back that I needed to be happy with what I had."

My uncle walked in silence for a time, for most of a mile at least. He was a methodical sort, and I knew he liked to chew things over before speaking most times. "Well, I think you need to get out of town for a bit."

"How you figure that?"

HD shrugged. "Won't anyone here teach you any spells. And I can't do more than learn you some sigils. So unless you can figure out how to make Krista come up off some more know-how, you need to get out, find someone who will."

What he said made sense in a way. He knew more about all this than me, using knowledge to compensate for a lack of ability. Those who can't do, teach, they say, and Hubert Dale had made a study of all this as best he could. "You may be right. Though not having a car kinda puts a damper on that. Well, that and not having a fucking clue about anyone with the gift outside of the county."

"Well, you got time to figure all that out. Master what's in that grimoire, start saving some pennies to get yourself a car, and in a year or two you'll be ready, I reckon."

"What, don't fancy a road trip?" I asked with a laugh.

HD grunted but didn't say anything. He just kept walking, mud pulling at his boots, me trailing a few feet behind. I just kept slapping at flies and mosquitos and let the man think. I didn't have any real proof, but I had long suspected HD was scared of leaving the county. Most folks, they had business that took them to Montgomery at some point or other. Him? Never. That van of his only ever set tire to roads inside the county, near as I could ever remember. He'd never even gone up to Montgomery, I didn't think.

"Maybe I'll be able to help track you down something cheap and reliable. I'll keep my eyes open." Clearly he was gonna ignore my comment, so I just let it ride.

I shook my head. "I mean you can keep your eyes open, but I wouldn't get my hopes up if I were you. Something I could afford, it ain't gonna be reliable. Unless you talking a matchbox car or the like."

"Yeah," said HD slowly. "Be that as it may, I think it's a plan. Main thing here is, I think you're headed in the right direction. We keep it smart, and out of sight of Granny—least till you're strong enough she can't do something about it—and it'll be good."

"Well, glad my newfound motivation has got your seal of approval," I said, wiping a smear of blood on my jeans. "Fingers crossed that it lasts awhile. I don't know . . ." It wasn't real easy for me to talk about feelings and crap like that. Definitely not my wheelhouse. I reckoned it all boiled down to Anna—not that I would ever admit it to her, or anyone else. She was one of the good ones, and damned if it hadn't motivated me to be a touch better.

Not too much better, though. I liked to keep a low bar.

"Well, you know I'm here if you need me. Tomorrow, maybe we dive on deep into that book, break out the dry erase board."

"Yeah, that's sorta what I was thinking for today, least before all this—" I started before HD raised a hand and cut me off.

"Fuck," was all he said.

Stepping around from behind him I saw green leaves splashed with crimson, beneath which sat a pale-skinned severed arm.

NEW ORLEANS GOODBYE

We had to walk back to the Camp before we could get enough signal on HD's cell to call the cops. It took the ambulance about an hour after that to eventually find the place, followed after by a trio of sheriffs' cars. Which was no comfort to me. The sheriff's office and I historically have had a somewhat antagonistic relationship.

By the time we led them out to the body it was well after lunch time, and I was starting to come down from the bulk of my drugs. In short, it was leaving me in a pissy mood, and I was making little move to hide it.

Sheriff Snow, the man who was in the running for most hated person on my list alongside Agent Rutherford, hitched up his pants beneath his ponderous belly. The walk out to the body had likely been the most exercise the fat man had done in years, and fifteen minutes later he was still red-faced and sweating.

Snow walked over to where HD and I were standing. His breathing was thick and loud, as if he would spend the rest of the day trying to fully catch his breath. I took solace in the fact that he still had to walk back to his car at some point. Maybe he'd have a heart attack.

"Marsh, why is it anytime something fucking weird happens in this county, you are somewhere in the area?"

My eyes bulged. "You fucking with me? You can't think I did this!"

Snow's frown deepened. "Mighty defensive there, Marsh. But no, for once I don't think you're guilty. At least of the crime present. You're guilty as sin of God knows how many other crimes. But not murder. Least not yet."

I plastered on my smarmiest fake smile and gave a mocking bow. "Your confidence in me leaves me weak, Sheriff."

"Quit while you're ahead, boy," HD said from beside me softly. He'd had a few run-ins with Snow over the years as well. Hell, it was practically a family tradition at this point. I just had turned it from tradition to a way life.

"Listen to your uncle, Marsh. Now, it's pretty clear it was an animal attack. Probably wild dogs. Did you two see anything? Hear anything? Coroner thinks it happened late yesterday, but I doubt they would have run off far."

I shook my head. HD said something, but I wasn't paying any attention. Snow mentioned wild dogs . . . what if it wasn't? My mind thought about a run I'd had with this Flicker Dog thing. What if it had been something like that instead? It looked like it could have easily wrecked that girl like that. Of course the odds of that were real low, but living a life like mine, you tend to assume the weirdest in any situation.

"Am I boring you, Marsh?" growled Snow.

I snapped out of my thoughts. "As usual, yeah."

The fat man glared at me and sucked his teeth angrily. "Get back to those tents and give your statement to one of my deputies. Then get the fuck out of here before I find a reason to lock you up."

He didn't wait for a response, just wheeled around and began barking orders at anyone who caught his eye. HD just shrugged and placed a hand on my shoulder. "Let's get out of here."

I let him pull me away, though I don't know why I felt so loathe to leave of a sudden. It certainly wasn't because of Snow; if anything, I wanted to get as far away from him as possible. I think I just knew that this Kandra chick was a lot more like me than the cops picking up her pieces. She needed someone there, one of her people—least that's what felt right to me. But orders was orders.

We began threading through the swamp, making our way back to the Camp. I was feeling antsy, and my stomach was growling, but at least the bugs seemed to have decided they had gotten all the little blood I had worth taking. I hoped they were off somewhere tripping to death on my drugged-up juices.

I waited until we were safely out of earshot of the cops behind before I started speaking. Still, I kept my voice low, just in case. "I keep thinking about that Flicker Dog."

HD nodded but held his tongue for a bit. My fingers were twitching, and for every two steps I was taking forward I was taking one or two to one side or the other. I was wired, and my brain was racing in a million directions at once. I didn't usually begrudge my uncle his slow thinking, but at that moment I could have choked the words up outa him.

"You got rid of it, though. And the odds of that happening a second time . . . well, it just don't add up. It was just wild dogs, and sad as that is, you know that."

He was right, but this was too goddamned senseless. There had to be something there. "Yeah, but—"

He held up his hand to cut me off. He kept quiet for a good long while till I was damn near fit to explode. Finally, though, after a minute that was closer to an eternity, he opened his mouth. "Now, like I said, this was just dogs. Maybe some sort of black bear come up from Florida or something. But just a regular animal. But … now, I'm only gonna mention this because of where we are."

"In a swamp. What's that got to do with it?"

HD gestured behind us. "If memory serves, not too far away from where that girl died, Morgan had a witch house where she did most of her spell work."

Morgan, the woman we were pretty sure had spelled up the curse that summoned the Flicker Dog in the first damn place. "Why can't I ever remember this fucking Morgan character?"

He shrugged. "You were young, it happens. I promise you she was real; you just don't remember her. You called her Auntie Morgan, and she was around all the time when you was little, learning from your grandparents. She took more to my dad, though, so when he … well, your granny ran her off. But she was quite the skilled little briar witch."

"So what, Kandra there stumbled across some ward or trap she left behind?" It'd be one hell of a ward to leave behind, but it wasn't totally unheard of.

"It's just wild dogs and bad luck." HD paused. "Morgan, she wasn't cruel. She could get mean, could get angry and all fired up. But she wasn't ever cruel; it's why she and Mom never got on. She could have left wards up—in fact, she'd have been a fool not to, and she weren't ever a fool. But that would have been damn nasty of her to leave behind for just any random folk to walk into. Cruel, even."

"Where'd she go when Granny ran her off?" HD was a notoriously bad judge of female character, I had learned from his string of ex-wives, so his opinion of what a Granny-trained briar witch may or may not do was somewhat suspect in my eyes.

"I don't know. No one does, as far as I know. She hasn't been back, though. Least, if she has, she's kept a real low profile."

I grunted. That meant exactly fuck all, then. She could be dead in a ditch, or camped out somewhere in the county lying low, or half a world away. Not knowing where the woman who was in a roundabout way responsible for damn near killin' me back in that Flicker Dog debacle was didn't exactly make for peaceful sleep at night.

"Boy, don't go chasing after ghosts that like as not ain't even there. You're in a pretty good place right now. Don't fuck it up by getting distracted with shit that don't concern you. Let's say it was Morgan what did that back there. So what? It's a shitty thing, but you ain't the problem solver for the whole damn county. Let the cops do what they do. Unless Rutherford comes knocking, just leave it be and focus on you." My uncle looked over at me, arching an eyebrow. "Now I've said my piece. You just need to think it through. Maybe more time thinking, less time drugging it up."

I rolled my eyes but held my tongue, which was quite a feat. HD was no stranger to the more illicit substances in life, having partaken many a time with yours truly. But he did love to tell a man how to run his life, if given half a chance. Preachy bastard.

As we walked I stewed on it, the fingers of both hands tapping against my thighs. I was all manner of twitchy, and I would rather have been talking it out but I could tell when HD was in one of his moods, so I saved my breath. Anyone else, I would have jawed their ear off just to piss them off. But I'm not famous for having a deep bench of friends to call on for rides and such, so I erred on the side of discretion. I was already walked out for the day.

The Camp came into view a bit later, now with the added colors of flashing cop lights. They clashed with the painted wildflowers, not that it mattered. One of the deputies that had been left behind was a very distant cousin of ours, though in truth, in Jubal County everyone was related in some way if you dug deep enough. Deputy Will was as close to a friendly face as existed amongst the local police, though, so we traipsed over to him to give our statements.

HD was close to done, and I had finished when the old church van that Johnny and Emily used to haul the band around pulled up. Before it was fully stopped, Emily had jumped from the passenger seat and was running over toward us, shouting my name.

Inwardly I cringed. This was going to suck.

Ghosts

"**M**arsh, HD, we can't thank you enough," Johnny was saying through our van window. He leaned in on the driver's side, his handsome face lined with worry. "And I'm so sorry . . ."

Uncle Hubert Dale put a hand on the man's arm. "No need."

Johnny let out a ragged sigh. "I need to get back to Emily. She's a wreck right now. You know how protective she gets." He wiped at his eye with a quick flick of his hand, then straightened. As he did, you could see a change wash over him. His eyes were dry and he looked solid, like a rock you could cling to in a rough time. He'd changed, just like that, into what his wife needed him to be. It was almost magic. Hell, maybe it was.

"Tomorrow, come back out. We are gonna throw a remembrance for Kandra, a wake in the old way. Wouldn't be right without you two there."

"We'll be there," HD said before I could respond.

"Good," Johnny said, extending his hand out to shake ours. We took it in turn, then he was gone.

"I'm not real big on the idea of coming back out here for a wake," I said. "Wake like that will run all night, at least, and I ain't real big on funerals and such. You know that."

"Well that is a pity, seeing as you are damn sure gonna be here iff'n I have to drag you behind the van to make it happen," said HD as he started the van and began backing out.

"Fuck you."

"You want my help tomorrow working through that grimoire, don't you? Then you're gonna have to come with me to this wake. Deal?"

"Goddamn it," I muttered.

"Yep," he said, turning onto the narrow track that led back to the main road.

A pain was developing into a headache behind my eyes. "And you aren't gonna help me otherwise?"

"Not tomorrow, at least," he grinned.

"Did I mention how I'm finally all motivated to learn?"

He laughed. "All the more incentive then to have your loving Professor Uncle by your side to help work through the tricky bits, then, I reckon."

In that moment I could have gleefully killed him, but knowing that smarmy bastard, he'd have counted that as some sort of twisted victory. And he'd probably haunt my ass, in all the most annoying ways possible.

I swear, one day my family will be the death of me. Not that some parts of it hadn't already tried, of course. But still.

The haggling went back and forth for most of the ride back. In the end I agreed to go, but he had to buy me a Blizzard and a small cone for Horace, my possum. I knew the little critter had likely missed me, so I decided that some fresh, unmelted ice cream for a change might make amends.

I was correct, as when I walked over from the Dairy Queen toward my home Horace came waddling out from behind the dumpster. He tried to act a little aloof, I think, but that went right out the window when I lowered the cone down to his height. I swear his eyes swelled up big as some anime girl's. The sound of him smacking away was a happy one as I made my way into my shed.

When the last of my Blizzard was gone I settled back into my chair and dug out my box of oblivion. I opened her up and just sat there gazing with lust-filled eyes at the array of treats before me. It was enough to almost bring a tear to my eye.

I thought back to that morning, and how I woke up in a puddle of my own drool, and decided that maybe I would stay away from the downers for now. And though I had a few snippets that would do to keep me up the rest of the week or so, I decided that I was feeling in the mood to get at least *some* sleep tonight. So in the end, I rolled a fat joint and popped a couple of tabs of some pretty high-grade acid. For someone like me, someone with the Power, LSD had the added effect of making your brain a bit more in tune with the world of spirits and such. It made for some almighty trippy experiences.

I let the blue ink stain my tongue and began taking hits off the weed. I thought that maybe I should have opted for the little bit of shrooms I had, but it was too late at that point, so I just leaned deeper into my chair and waited for the drugs to take me away. Fumbling around without looking, I managed to click my old CD player on. It whirred to life, and Donovan began humming along faintly from the speakers.

This was a CD Krista had burned me a few years ago, mostly oldies with a little jam rock mixed in. It had become my favorite album to smoke out to, and so it rarely left my rotation. I let the music wash over me and closed my eyes, taking it all in.

I knew things were getting right when the music began to take on a particular richness tonally. I began hearing notes that may well have not been there, or were but I'd just never been in the correct mental state to notice. "Hurdy Gurdy Man" was tickling my ears in all manner of new ways as the LSD settled in to work its magic.

When I opened my eyes again some minutes later, the drugs had firmly taken hold. The yellow bulb that lit my shed had taken on a pulsing vibe that swirled around the corners of my vision. I raised my hand and slowly passed it before my eyes, and my arm left a sea of contrails in its wake.

The music felt like fingertips gently trailing across my skin. I felt warm and connected, a peace flowing from my heart to my toes. The colors of my room were brighter and more crisp, the gray of the tin roof having gone silver and glowing. Moonlight pooled on the ground outside in quicksilver puddles, ebbing and flowing as clouds passed overhead.

I knew none of it was real, just the acid warping my perception, but it was beautiful. For a while I would be able to forget the ugly filth that surrounded me, the chains and ties that bound me. My face split in a smile wide enough to swallow the whole world, and mercifully I spared the Earth that fate.

I was a god, but a just one.

Impulsively I leapt from my chair. I was tired of the smoky yellows that bathed me, and I wanted to dance in the cool colors of night. Gravel crunched beneath my shoes and I could taste it, taste the sound. It bathed my tongue with a dry, earthy flavor that made me think of fallen leaves.

White gold drenched my skin as around me the night eddied and whirled. I found myself laughing, but I didn't know why. My voice sounded distant, like it was coming from a deep hole within me, echoing up from an infinite nowhere.

"Marsh," warbled Corey. "Shut up."

I spun and there he was, standing in the doorway of his shed. His eyes were glowing an incandescent green, and I could see the thin red trails that his words had left as they flowed out his mouth. Puffy clouds of light billowed from around him, and he looked like nothing so much as some primitive aerial god of yore.

My words threaded toward him in strings of blue that faded to a crystalline white in the moonlight. "Corey. I love you, man."

His green, glowing eyes rolled, and with a snort like thunder he returned to his domain. My heart was full for the fat little god in the shed down from mine, and I thought about going and telling him that. I'd even taken a few steps to do so when a smell assailed my nostrils.

It was the scent of the grave.

Slowly I turned, an ache of fear starting to blossom in that infinite well inside me. I didn't want to look, longing to close my eyes, but perverse curiosity kept them open. And then there she was.

Parts of Kandra were still missing, enough that she shouldn't have been able to stand there. Half her face was shredded to the bone, and one eye dangled from a crushed socket. Blood black as tar spread from around her feet, so dark it looked like she might fall into it at any moment.

LSD doesn't cause hallucinations—it just alters your perception of reality. I knew that. So that meant that she was really there, or at least her spirit was. I was frozen with fear, unable to even begin to think of what I should be doing.

She screamed then. It wasn't angry, wasn't filled with rage. It was a cry of sadness tinged with bitter frustration. I could see the torrent of colors exploding from her mouth, sultry crimsons and deep purples. She tilted her head back and vented her poison, and it filled the sky like ink poured into water.

It went on longer than any human lungs could have produced. It clouded the moon, hiding its blue-silver glow with thick clouds of amaranthine sorrow. Unspoken words rained down from above, pitter-pattering hotly onto my skin. A scene filled my mind.

I could smell the swamp, taste the fear, feel the pain. I saw glimpses of black fur on pale skin painted red with blood. I felt a heart stop, and mine stopped with it in sympathy.

I fell to my knees, gasping for breath and pounding my chest. My bulging, fear-filled eyes watched powerless as the word rain puddled on the ground. Tiny green shoots sprouted, then shot up into thorny vines which wrapped around my arms. Sharp pricks twisted and dug into the skin of my wrists, tearing and ripping my flesh. I tried to scream, but I couldn't get air into my lungs.

I was losing consciousness, and fast. My vision was fading to black, and the strength was fast bleeding from my limbs. I could only watch helplessly as Kandra stepped close and, raising one ragged stump, smeared blood across my forehead.

And then I knew only blackness.

WELL THEN

I was surprised when I woke up. I had been pretty sure I was dying in those last few moments, but unless hell was oddly similar to the Elk Grove hospital, I was still kicking. I had mixed feelings about that.

My chest ached something fierce, and there was a fiery feeling in my wrists. Looking down I could see that both arms were tightly wrapped in bandages. They were both also handcuffed to the rails of the bed. "Fuck me."

"Marsh?" came a sleep-bleary voice from across the room. I turned my head and saw Krista sitting there, curled up in a chair, a blanket across her. She rose from her seat, wiping the sleep from her eyes, concern written large across her face. The faintest golden glow coming from her eyes told me that the LSD hadn't fully cleared from my system yet.

"What happened?" I asked in a croak. My throat was hoarse and dry, and I could see where some asshole had put a glass of water nearby. How they expected me to grab it with my hands cuffed was beyond me. Probably one of the nurse's idea of a joke. I'd dated a couple over the years, so that would be about par for the course.

"Mr. Davis said you were . . . acting weird . . ."

"Tripping balls."

She frowned. I could see the faint whiff of her annoyance lurking down deep, but she was wanting to feel sad and pity my imagined circumstance at the moment, so I resolved to goad her right out of that.

"Acting weird. He said when you got suddenly real quiet, he got nervous so he looked out and saw you lying on the ground. He ran over, but your heart had stopped. He did CPR on you."

Pudgy little Davis had saved my life! That was unexpected. I certainly owed him one. A big one. I might even pay up one day.

"When you were breathing again he called 9-1-1. And now you're here. You have a couple cracked ribs—"

"I guess from Tubs pressing down on my chest?"

Krista slapped my arm, then flinched as I flinched. "Shit, sorry," she gasped, then she remembered why she'd done it in the first place. Watching her face cycle from annoyance to sorrow and back made my morning. She settled on annoyance, thankfully. "He saved your life, Marsh!"

"Maybe a few less pork rinds and he'd have saved it without splitting my chest open," I snarked.

She threw her hands up. "I don't know why I was concerned, you ass. Jesus, you're impossible."

"Yeah, yeah. So why the cuffs?"

Her frown returned. "Because you tried to kill yourself. Cut your wrists."

I snorted. "You know good and well those days are past. I'd tell you how I got those, but I don't really want to, and you might not believe me anyway. Now give me some water."

She stared at me for a moment, then grabbed the cup and held it to my lips. I'll never be able to prove it, but I am almost positive she held it just that way so that most would spill down my chin. That would be something she'd do.

"They gonna cut me loose now?" I asked, my throat feeling much better now.

"You're welcome. And they are prepared to turn you loose if someone will sign for you, basically. And somehow I wound up as your emergency contact"—she glared at me at that point—"so they'll let me do it."

I stared at her blankly. "Then shoo, go sign papers, let's get. Lots to do today."

I am pretty sure her brain broke in that moment. Luckily it fixed itself, but I could see as it rebooted a couple of times in rapid succession. Her mouth kept opening to say something, then closing. In the end, she just turned and walked out of the room.

It's hard being me sometimes.

I Saw the Sign

Leaning back, I took a gander at my handiwork. "How's that?"

HD got up from my chair and took a look at the sigil I had drawn. I'd copied it over from the grimoire I had taken off Brandt. In fact I'd copied it about a dozen times now, maybe a touch more. In truth I had gotten the pattern of it down pretty solid about six etchings ago, but HD wanted me to be sure.

"Well, I reckon you've got it. Slap it up there, and we can call it a day. Getting close to time to head out to the Camp anyways." He settled back into my chair, beer in hand as he watched me.

I took a deep breath, and taking up the little paintbrush I climbed up on top of the minifridge, kneeling on it and being careful to not hit my bandaged wrists on anything. Being short, I needed something to get me up high enough to paint the sigil where it needed to go. And if I did it right, the day wouldn't be wasted.

It was mostly HD that had come up with what all he'd had me throw up on the walls. Brandt's book didn't have anything too out there, nothing HD hadn't seen before—or at least a variation of, that is. What it had done was show him a few combinations that hadn't crossed his mind, but none of that were particularly useful for what we was trying to do.

Most of the glyphs, they would work to keep my place off the map, so to speak, when it came to magical spying. I wasn't sure if Granny ever cared enough to check in on me, but if she was trying, this in theory would keep her out of my business. More likely was anyone else running around out there that might want to keep an eye on me, like Preach . . . which was a very pressing worry of mine. I knew I had to make things right there, but being me, I had been avoiding the problem in hopes it would go away. But someone had left a pulled pork sandwich on my stoop last week, which was bizarrely ominous.

Only in the county would threats come via pork products.

I was still trying to decipher just what it meant that it'd had no sauce on it. Did that make it more threatening? Less? I was on the fence. The sandwich had been good, though, if a bit dry.

Anyway, a few of them glyphs though would work to warn me if supernatural-type stuff had got inside my place or was getting real close. It might be enough to give me an edge if something went to attack me, enough warning to get a spell or two ready. At least that was the plan.

Really, a lot of it was a good bit beyond me skillswise. I was fairly surprised to learn that there was more to sigil making than just drawing it out and infusing a bit of magic. That would have been too easy, of course, and nothing in my life was easy, ever.

Squinting hard, I began moving the brush in slow, careful strokes. Not only did I have to make them look right, but I had to do each stroke in a certain order while thinking particular thoughts, flooding in certain feels of Power. It was sorta like juggling balls while trying to recite poetry.

On the smaller, less important sigils that lined the tops of my walls, it hadn't been that hard. They worked more from sheer number than complexity. But this one, this was gonna tie it all together and kinda power the whole shebang. There were sigils in that book that could power themselves and do all kinds of cool shit. But it was gonna take a disturbing amount of practice to get even one of those down if this fairly simple little number was any sort of example.

If all went well, this little glyph was gonna tie itself into the pair of skulls I kept on my back wall. The cow skull, with what I was pretty sure was a comatose Flicker Dog inside, was gonna act as a battery. And the deer skull, with its Granny-inscribed sigils, was gonna act as a little bit of extra protection from her watching in. Again, I wasn't sure exactly how it worked, but that's what I had HD for.

Bastard had spent about two decades researching sigils that he couldn't even make himself. And if he couldn't walk me through this, then I don't think anyone else was gonna. Not like I had a long list of teachers lined up, after all.

With the last stroke I realized I'd mostly been holding my breath. I sent the last pulse of Power in and the sigil glowed to life, a flare of red. I climbed down and stepped back, turning slowly. All around the room, up near the ceiling, a long row of tiny sigils flared to life, one after the other. From the eyes of the skulls, red light started shining out as well. Then gradually they all faded away so that I would have to use my little magic revealing spell to see them again . . . or if something triggered them.

"Guess that means I did it right . . ." I muttered.

HD was standing up as well, and with a grin he looked over at me. "I guess you did. Hopefully you don't ever need to find out, but come the day, I reckon you'll be in good shape, boy."

It had been a long, long time since my chest had swelled with pride. And the coughing fit my smoker's lungs blessed me with cut it short. But that good feeling filled me right up as I stared up at what I'd managed.

Goddamn, it felt good.

THE KEENING

It was night, but it wasn't dark in the Camp. The generator was pumping and dozens of strings of lights lit the night air. Kerosene lanterns, the usual form of lighting here, hung from poles and trees every few feet, and at the highest point of the little knoll a large fire blazed.

I kept having little acid flashbacks, brief moments where the idly flapping tarps would shift and spin or the lights would flare and churn with new colors. In those moments I would freeze, standing still until they passed. It was like tremors after an earthquake, tiny ripples that morphed my vision.

A couple dozen folks were dancing around the fire, spinning in time to Johnny's fiddle music as Emily sang. I'd done a few turns around the blaze, but my smoke-addled lungs weren't as young as they used to be, so I settled down with a Mason jar of 'shine that someone had produced and resolved to get pretty damn drunk. At the first sip, I could tell it was some of my daddy's making. I hated the man, but he made good brew.

Off to one side they had hung a window from a tree limb. The glass had long ago been broken out of it, and there was of course no wall there, but they had still opened it. According to the old ways, Kandra's spirit would pass through it to find the other side. Someone had duct taped a trio of fat candles on its frame, the thinking being the candles would snuff out when she passed.

All three blazed happily.

Kandra's spirit was far too angry to pass through that window—that much I knew. She'd hang around until I'd gotten her some revenge. So unless the wind picked up, those candles would burn till they burned themselves out.

The music eased to a stop, and HD plopped down on the bench beside me. His cheeks were flush from dancing. For being a good fifteen or so years older than me, he could outdance most of us young folks with ease.

"It's drawing on midnight!" called Johnny from the makeshift stage he'd been playing on. "Emily and I, we wrote Kandra a song to ease the passing. To show her we love her. We figured we'd play it now, with the witchin' hour getting close."

Emily, pulling an errant strand of hair back behind her ear, stepped a little forward. "Sorry, guys, this ain't a dancing song."

Then Johnny began to play. And the little bit of magic he had in him shone through, bright enough that even those without the gift had to be left wondering just a little bit. For me and HD he was like a lantern in the dark.

The fiddle loosed long, mournful notes, pouring out a river of sorrow and regret. He hadn't been playing but a score of seconds before tears started welling up in my eyes, and I could see I wasn't alone in that. An awed hush fell over the Camp, people barely daring to breathe lest they miss so much as a note.

Emily joined in then. She didn't sing in words, just an aria of a sadness-tinged voice. Her voice threaded and weaved through the fiddle's notes, blending into a perfect mesh. Through it all, though, one feeling came through more powerful than the ache of loss: love.

An echo of the LSD hit me then, and the music became a visual phenomenon. The sounds became a giant storm cloud of dark colors. Purples and dark blues bloomed into existence, while with every high note Emily crooned soaring reds would part the clouds.

I froze as I saw Kandra appear. She floated there above the pair, hovering a dozen feet up. I glanced around, and no one else could see her, it seemed, just me. I could only watch in horror as she drifted down, arms spread wide.

Then the LSD flashback faded. I swore under my breath and began muttering a few words under my breath. There are ways to see spirits that don't involve drugs; they just take Power. I felt an electric spark flow up from my heart to my eyes, and then everything had a greenish tint.

Kandra was right above the pair now. Instead of attacking, though, she was just hovering there, looking as though she wanted nothing more than to scoop them up in a massive hug. As the music played, the ragged wounds that covered her body began to heal. Wounds closed, and missing parts reformed with each passing note.

Emily stepped down from the stage, never stopping her wordless song. She walked around the gathered folk, taking each woman in hand, creating a chain of females locked arm in arm. Like a snake eating its tail, she led them to circle the fire, then reached out to clasp the last woman in the string's free hand.

I could see a few of the women knew what was happening, but most had no idea, only going along because of their trust in Emily. I knew, though. This was a ceremony in the old way, and Emily was set to do a Keening. Crying out for the dead.

Kandra, as fully healed as she was fully dead, had floated over to above the fire. As she drew closer, her mark on my forehead began to ache slightly, a not too subtle reminder of my task.

"In the old days, they performed the Keening," Johnny said as Emily grew silent. He continued to play, but slower, his tone more muted. "The women would wail, so the dead knew they were not forgotten. So they could ride those cries into the hereafter."

I wasn't sure how true that was, but I wasn't going to argue.

Emily began to cry out. It was a long, haunted wail that soared up through the overhanging limbs. Those women who had been a part before joined in, their voices loosing cries of their own. Soon, the entire circle was screaming up at the heavens and, though they didn't realize it, right at Kandra.

The spirit began to fade, gazing directly at me as she did. My forehead pulsed, and I nodded toward her. I wouldn't forget. I wasn't sure if she was passing on, made suddenly less vengeful by the outpouring of love, or just going away for the moment. I knew my luck, though; I figured she'd be back.

The candles were still burning. A twist of my fingers and a few choice words, and they flicked out. May as well make someone happy that night—let them think they'd really done something.

Grave Concerns

We left soon after. The dancing and singing would go on all night, but we had plans for the morning, and while I am always one to ignore my responsibilities in the name of a good time, my ride was not. He'd sweated out most of the beer he'd drank while dancing, so if anything he was more sober leaving than he was when he'd arrived.

I was as blue as the night was dark. Nothing like going to a wake to leave you wondering who would show up at your funeral. The way things were, I suspected it might be a small handful of family, maybe my drug dealer. Rutherford would probably show up later to piss on my grave, if he could muster up the care. Snow would probably throw a party. Hell, there would be more people there to make sure I was really dead than to celebrate my shit life.

Unless Krista came into some money, I was pretty sure that I wouldn't even get a headstone in the family plot. HD would likely whittle something up, but there would be no rock, nothing that wouldn't just rot away. Maybe Uncle Rooster would spring for one if it crossed his mind, though that wasn't likely.

It's hard to be lonely when you are surrounded by people, but I did a pretty passable job of it. The only way to be happy in a place like Jubal County is to embrace it, to embrace the people, to meld into the masses and not stand out too much. Small-town Alabama is not the place for unique self-expression.

I couldn't do all that, though. I'd seen what hides behind that facade of the moral majority. In a way, you could say I embraced all the real values of the county; I just didn't have the decency to hide it like everyone else. Either way, I couldn't live like them, and I couldn't stand to be a part of them. Drugs were the only way I managed.

HD sighed as I began rummaging around in my little box of oblivion. "Shit's gonna kill you one day, boy."

I shrugged and just kept digging. If the space inside the box was a little bigger than the outside of it would lead you to believe, well, that just had to be an optical illusion. I had to sleep tonight, but if I was gonna bed down only a house or so away from Granny's, I was gonna need to be fucked up.

"You hear me?" HD said, his voice hard.

I popped a couple of pills and chased them with a swig of one of the last beers. "Yeah, just trying to ignore you. Not gonna have this conversation for the hundredth time. Not tonight."

HD huffed but held his tongue the rest of the way to his house. He lived on the same hill as Granny and a couple of other family members in the middle of several hundred acres that constituted the ancestral holdings. Before the Civil War, it had been one of the largest plantations in the county. Granny still made the old mansion her home, though like everything else my family touched, it had seen far better days.

The lights were off at the old mansion, which meant nothing. Granny was just as prone to creeping around in the dark as light. Knowing her, she was prolly hunched in front of her bedroom window watching us drive by—not that I'd be able to see her without a touch of magic, and I wasn't fool enough to try that on the old biddy.

The van pulled into the driveway of HD's small home. In silence we staggered on mostly steady feet onto his porch, having to use the handrail a bit more than two fully sober folks might would have needed. My uncle fumbled a bit with the knob, his key struggling to find the slot.

Then he grunted—and froze. Cocking his head as though trying to listen to a distant noise, I saw a sour look cross his face. He stood like that for several seconds, utterly silent.

"What is it?" I hissed.

He turned his head to look at me with narrow, angry eyes. "It's a good thing I wasn't trying to listen or anything, what with you jawin' on." Turning back, he opened the door and stepped inside. "Sleep light. I think something's coming."

I stared at his back as he threw his keys on the table. "Care to expand on 'something'? Or just gonna be all ominous and mysterious as usual?"

He slumped onto his leather couch. His house was mostly just one big room that was both a living room and kitchen with only a bathroom and bedroom separate down a tiny hall. The whole place was disgustingly clean and tidy, far too much so for my tastes. My uncle was a piss-poor bachelor.

"If I knew, I'd tell you, smartass," he said, pulling off his boots. "Just a gut feeling. Something's coming this way, and it ain't a good something."

I knew well enough to trust the man's hunches. The Power often skipped generations, but in the ones it skipped there were often echoes and traces of it still flowing. At this point in my life, HD's gut was the most trustworthy thing in my family.

The pills I had taken were starting to make me drowsy, and I knew in a few minutes I would be out like a rock. "Sleep light, gotcha."

He rummaged up his remote and clicked on the TV. "You can take the bed tonight. I'm gonna conk out here on the couch, I think. Pretty damn beat."

I knew he kept a shotgun hid under that couch. I also knew he wouldn't sleep a wink until whatever it was showed its face. We were quite the bunch of liars. But his mattress was calling, and I wasn't gonna argue.

I awoke to a slap across my face, hard enough to set my jaw aching. I launched myself up, arm raised to start throwing punches, but a firm hand caught my wrist. As my bleary eyes gained focus, I could see HD staring back at me. I quit struggling, snatching my arm back as his grip loosened. "The fuck was that for?"

HD was holding the shotgun in his other hand. He stalked over to the nearest window, pulling the blinds slightly apart. "You wouldn't wake up. It's here."

I crawled off the bed and padded over on bare feet to beside him. I was awake, but I was not thinking clearly.

My brain was still in a fog from my drug induced sleep; I felt like I was moving in slow motion. "What's here? What fucking time is it?"

"Three a.m.," he said, glancing at his watch. "And I don't know yet. But I think something is creeping around the edge of the wards."

The hillside was covered with all manner of wards, put up over the years by Granny and sometimes her apprentices. HD couldn't make them himself, but he'd always been fascinated by them, so had studied them as much as he could without drawing Granny's attention.

"If it's coming on the hill, it ain't coming for us," I said, rubbing at my eyes, trying to get them to start focusing properly. "It'll go for Granny.

He grunted. "I can't see shit from here. I'm going on the porch."

I debated crawling back into the bed, but I knew I would never hear the end of it if I did. I mean, best case scenario for me would be if this something killed the old bitch. But I knew I wouldn't be that lucky, and besides, anything strong enough to kill her would be bad fucking news. So sluggishly I followed him out. I thought about pulling on my shoes, but that just seemed like such a daunting task that I said fuck it.

It was just cool enough outside that I wished I had bothered to put my shirt back on. It wasn't spring weather yet, but just close enough that tell it was coming. So there was a definite chill in the air, and I now really regretted not going back to bed. I'd rather have dealt with HD's bitching. Too late now, though, I reckoned.

The night was dark, and what moonlight there should have been was obscured by clouds. There was a security light over on the far side of the hill, by my Uncle Mike's house, but that was several hundred yards away. There was no other light to be seen, and I quickly established that we were looking at nothing.

I was about to write off my uncle as a loon, in spite of his track record, and go back inside. I had actually turned to do so when I felt the faint pulse. It was like someone striking a very tiny match in a dark room—very faint, but in total darkness you could get a peek of light. Nearby, someone had used the Power to take out a ward. If I hadn't been awake, I'd never have known. "Fuck me," I muttered.

"What?" HD asked.

I stepped to the porch railing, staring in the direction I had felt the pulse. "You were right. Someone just took out a ward."

He worked the pump on the shotgun. The ratcheting sound was loud, grating against my ears.

I caught a glimpse of movement, shadow on shadow. It was so quick I couldn't be sure I had even seen it. And with the repeated acid flashbacks I had been having, it's not like I could really trust my eyes. I should have said something, but in my brain fog it never even crossed my mind. I just kept watching the same spot to see if it would repeat itself.

Suddenly wards began popping off in rapid-fire succession up the hillside, straight for the looming hulk of Granny's house. These weren't being snuffed out—they were being triggered. Light pulsed on the hillside now, blue-white flashes color that made me blink involuntarily. Beside me my uncle cried out, though his shout was mostly covered by the shrieking sound of warning wards going off.

In the midst of the crackling lights I saw a black shadow racing past. It was making a beeline for the old woman's home, no longer bothering to try and approach in secret. I wasn't sure why, but the thing had decided that speed now trumped stealth.

It was a panther. Had my mind been clearer, I'd like as not have realized it right off the bat. "Panther!" I yelled at HD and pointed to where I'd seen it, as though he couldn't see all the wards being triggered.

He was running into the yard, shotgun held to his shoulder. Cursing, I took off after him, instantly regretting it as my bare feet hit the gravel of his drive. I knew I would have some bad bruises in the morning, but the brain fog served one good purpose: For the moment, it dulled the sharper edges of the pain.

I managed to catch the man as he stopped to try and take a shot. I snatched him back and spun him around. "Get in the fucking house, you old fuck! Spells are about to start fucking flying!"

His face twisted. He knew I was right, but it ate him, not being able to help. We all hated Granny, but she was ours to hate, not anyone else's. I pulled the shotgun from his grip. "House, now!"

With a snarl he started walking slowly backwards. I knew he'd go inside and dig out another gun in a minute, but I just had to hope it would be over by then.

The sky exploded with color as, behind me, a spell struck the ward protecting the mansion. I turned to see crackling flame slide down the invisible dome of the protection ward, and a scream of rage filled the night air. I felt Power thick in the air, easily more than I could muster. Gritting my teeth, I wished I had had time to dive into my box of oblivion and fuel up. I'd be going in light, and with a sluggish brain at that.

I never saw myself dying for Granny. By Granny's hand, sure. But *for* her?

"Fuck it," I said, and I started running up the hill.

Just a Shot in the Dark

Luckily I got onto grass pretty quickly. I'd spent most of my youth barefoot, and more than your normal person as an adult, so I had enough calluses that so long as a rock or stick didn't jab me, I would be alright. I still felt like I was running through thick soup, but at least it was progress.

The flames had pooled at the base of the dome, igniting the grass in a half circle around the house. Normally invisible, the ward prevented magic from passing through. Whoever it was shaped into that panther, they would have to come out of that form if they wanted inside.

I could feel Granny gathering up Power inside. She burned like a bonfire in my mind's eye, but for her to strike back, she was going to have to either come out or take down the ward. I myself had no idea what she'd do, so I just carried on with my plan to put some buckshot in that panther.

I ratcheted the pump on the gun and watched as a shell ejected out the side. I was so drug addled I'd forgotten that HD had pumped it once already. Cursing, I stopped and scooped up the shell and fed it back into the gun with fumbling fingers.

When I looked up, I could see that the magical flames had created real flames and that the grass inside the dome was burning, inching its way toward the house. Nothing I could do about that, so I started casting my eyes about for the panther. I only had so much Power, and I knew I needed to save as much as possible. I'd never really been taught anything defensive—why waste time teaching a tool you won't care about if it dies, being Granny's logic—so I had to go on the offensive.

The fire's crackling glow was providing enough light that I was able to see the panther dart in and strike the ward. Claws raked across the bubble in a shower of multicolored sparks. The big cat leapt back, yowling in pain as it did.

Inside the circle of protection, the fire snuffed out, just as earlier I had put out the wake candles. It dimmed the light to the point that I lost sight of the black shape. I was almost in range where the shotgun could actually do some good, so of course now I couldn't see.

Another spell launched itself out of the darkness to strike the ward. It felt like a shard of raw Power. It struck with enough force that for a moment the bubble shimmered and flickered as though it might fail.

It also cast a baleful glow over the area, which allowed me to see the cat.

I threw the shotgun to my shoulder and fired. I felt the kick, but I rolled my shoulder with it and began ratcheting in another round. The pellets kicked up a storm of dirt just beside the panther, and with a snarl it turned to face me.

Its narrowed eyes were glowing a faint golden color, and its teeth were eerily white in the spell-forged glow that bathed us. Did its eyes widen, and then narrow when it saw me? I wasn't sure, and I decided I would rather have a dead panther thing at my feet than an answer.

My first shot had been low, but I had my bearings now. I was a fair shot when I put my mind to it, and it being a shotgun, that certainly helped. Round fed, I dug deep and called up some of my Power. It had taken a fair bit of trial and error over the years, testing that had damn near cost me a couple fingers a time or two, but I'd figured out how much Power I could safely feed into a shell before it would explode on me.

I fired.

The pellets left streaks on my vision. Each tiny dot was a red-green shard that ripped through the night air like the leavings of a sparkler. It was like what I imagined tracer fire would look like, only prettier. It was a tiny Fourth of July celebration in a shell.

A few hit the ground around the creature, popping and hissing like water slung into hot grease. Most, though, peppered the hide of the kitty with a crackling sound. There was a smaller flash of light that went with it, indicating I had mostly struck warding or some type of shield. But the yowl that came ripping up out that cat's mouth let me know at least one pellet had struck home.

The panther leapt, springing into the air, head snapping back as though it was trying to bite the wound out of existence. It landed, its glowing eyes locked on mine. It made a move, a tensing of muscle that made it clear it was about to come eat my face clean off. So, I just racked in another shell and moved to take aim. I wasn't sure how many shots this thing had in it, but I was pretty sure it was at least one more after this.

Whatever this cat was, and clearly it had some sort of magic about it, it also had enough intelligence to realize I was locked and loaded. With a snarl it turned and began to race away into the night. The damn thing was quick, turning around quicker than I could have ever dreamed and putting paw to ground.

So I shot the thing in the ass.

Pellet streaks chased after it, a glow shining against the darkness. The creature was already out of sight but I heard another yowl of pain and, unable to stop myself, I cackled. Racking what was possibly my last round, I yelled out, "Here, kitty, kitty!"

The thing about wards, I was learning, is they are pretty sporty for stopping the brunt of magical attacks, or at least slowing them up. I, however, had no such wards running, so when the pulse of Power came out the gloom and struck me, I was woefully unprepared.

My last clear memory was flying back as an invisible force smacked me center mass. My head rocked back against the ground with enough force that I was down, my vision almost instantly fading to black.

Brain, Brain, Take Me on out of This Place

I was only fully out for a minute or so, maybe less. But my brain was scrambled, and I kept slipping under. Life was coming at me in a series of slides, and I wasn't real sure they were coming in any sort of actual order.

click

HD's face is looking down at me, all sorts of panic stricken. He's shaking me, asking if I'm alive, as though he can't see my eyes glaring up at him for jostling my head, which feels like it's filled with glass shards all of a sudden.

click

I hear a voice, one I haven't heard in a while. It's ancient sounding, filled with anger. I know Granny's voice when I hear it. I black out again, but I think more from fear than the concussion I probably have.

click

I'm being set back into bed. HD is muttering soft, encouraging phrases. I manage to mutter out a desire for bacon for when I wake up. I don't actually—I don't think, at least. It just seemed the thing to say.

click

Dawn was real faintly trying to shine through the window. I'd been asleep, not blacked out, I though. There was someone in the room with me, and I looked closer. It was Krista. She was standing by the window, standing real still and sorta peeking out secret like. I would have bet a dollar to a donut she was watching Granny's. I decided to just go back to sleep.

What the Hell Does "Bet a Dollar to a Donut" Mean?

I woke up when the pain in my head got too bad. I knew you ain't supposed to sleep with a concussion, and I knew my family knew that too. My guess is they weighed the option between letting me possibly die and forcing me to stay awake, something they knew damn well I probably drive them all nuts fighting.

Or maybe Granny just told them to leave me to die. She's a dear like that.

Some thoughtful soul had left a couple of Advil and a glass of water on the little nightstand. I wished they had been a little more thoughtful and dug into my little party box and pulled out something better than Advil, but that didn't stop me from downing them right fast. My head was pounding, and it was making my eyes squint up.

With a groan I shuffled out of bed and made my way into the main part of the house. As I entered, my uncle jumped up from the chair he was sitting in. He'd been hunched over the kitchen table, upon which sat a giant mound of cooked bacon.

"Hey, now, you should probably still be in bed. You took a hard hit." He had big dark bags under his eyes. I suspected he hadn't been to sleep at all and that worry had been eating him up. I decided to cut him a little slack for a change.

"Yeah, I'll take it easy. Mostly just up to get something stronger than Advil, is all." I gently rubbed my hand across the back of my head. There was a big ol' knot there, and fuck me if it didn't hurt to touch. I didn't feel any dried blood, though, or any gashes, so there was that, at least.

Tenderly, I sat down at the table in front of Mt. Bacon. On the one hand I knew I was hungry, but on the other I just didn't want to eat. For all the sense that made. I wondered why he'd cooked so much bacon. Was this some sort of guilt coping mechanism? Guilt bacon? I was befuddled but just couldn't muster up enough care to ask about it.

HD was rummaging through a drawer, looking at medicine bottles one after another. I figured he probably had some left over goodies, maybe some 'codone if I was lucky. He was usually not one for indulging my pill whims, but it seemed that actual injury was a worthy enough cause to break out the good stuff. "One sec, I think I got something here that'll help," he was muttering.

"While you're at it, how 'bout you fill me in on what the fuck happened?" I closed my eyes and cradled my head in my hand, low-key wishing for death. "But maybe talk real quiet like."

I heard the tiny clacking sound of pills hitting the table-top. Without opening my eyes I groped around blindly for them, my callused hand palming the wood. I found them quickly enough and popped them straight into my mouth, and with practiced ease I swallowed the two horse pills down without any liquid.

"Eat something with those, or your stomach is gonna hate you in a bit," he said softly. I heard him slide the plate of bacon closer to me. I blindly groped a piece to my mouth. Nice and crispy.

"Well, looks like Morgan came back. Least that's what your Granny is saying. Guess she was trying to get at Momma, take her out with surprise before the family could circle the wagons, so to speak. Don't reckon she counted on you, though. Must have put a kink in her gears, you peppering her hide with a juiced-up shotgun."

"You failed to mention that Morgan was a panther."

I could damn near hear the man's shrug. "I didn't know she could shape change. Only person I knew could do that was your Granny. Guess Morgan learned a bit, wherever she got off too."

I wasn't up to vocalizing my annoyance, so I just kept cool and spoke around a second piece of bacon. "So what's the plan, then? And where'd Krista get off to?"

"Huh? I ain't seen Krista. What're you talking about?"

I knew good and well I'd seen her but didn't want to argue it. "Must have been a dream, don't worry about it. So what's the plan?"

I finally cracked my eyes open a bit. HD was frowning at me, clearly not believing me but just as clearly sure that Krista, in fact, had not been there. I guess he decided to not address it, because he carried on as if I hadn't spoken.

"Well, your Granny said to just carry on as usual. That Morgan was after her, and she could take care of herself. She was kinda pissed at first that you got involved, 'cause she had a plan to take care of the bitch, she says, and you mucked it up. But I talked some sense into her."

"I figured we wouldn't have the good luck that the fire spread and burned her and that house of horrors all up," I said, finishing the last of the piece of bacon I'd slowly been working my way down.

"Don't talk like that, boy," my uncle growled. Granny was a righteous bitch, but I guess she was still HD's momma. And folks always have a blind spot for their momma. Not that I'd know from firsthand experience.

I waved my hand at him dismissively. "So just act like nothing happened. Right. You know she probably killed that girl, right?"

HD looked uncomfortable. "We don't know that."

I rolled my eyes, pretty much instantly regretting the fact as it sent a tiny wave of pain through my head. "Of course not. A woman no one's seen in decades shows up looking like a big cat, and around the same time someone gets tore up by a 'wild animal' right around this same mystery woman's old witch house. Total coincidence."

HD went to talk, but I cut him off. "Look, do me a favor and just run me home. I'm gonna close my door and not come out till this all blows over and my head feels right again. I ain't looking to get caught up in no shitstorm of Granny's, so I wanna be far away."

BLACK HOLE SUN

I did exactly as I said I was gonna. When I got back to my shed, a bit after lunchtime and with a pocket full of bacon, I called up Horace and closed my door. I had food and drink enough for a couple days and a bucket in the corner I could piss in if it came down to it. I was prepped and ready to hide.

Slumping onto the couch, I didn't bother to unfold it into a cot, it being just me there. I shot Anna a text to let her know I was pretty sure I was concussed but to not worry about me, that I was being looked after. It was a lie, but knowing her if I told her what was what, her nursing student ass would be here babying me something fierce.

I liked her—she was great—but just then all I wanted to do was sleep in the dark. I pulled the string on my light, and with the door to my shed closed, it was black as a gravedigger's heart. My good buddy Horace crawled up beside me and nestled into my gut, rootin' around until he was comfortable. I gave his fat belly a scratch and slipped him some bacon from my coat pocket.

I could hear him crunching away happily, and I was certain that I would be woke up at some point to the little bastard rooting into my pocket to get the rest. I had gotten a fucking soft spot for the prick, and I let the tubby bastard get away with damn near whatever he wanted. He had a little dog bed to sleep on, but so long as he wasn't too sticky with dumpster juices I would always just let him sleep alongside me.

I was pretty sure we were starting to share dreams on occasion. If not, something in my psyche had me trash diving in my dreams. I'd had this recurring dream of finding a whole, untarnished ice cream cake at the bottom of the DQ big green dumpster, and the things I found myself doing to it were kinda disturbing. Unseemly.

Horace was already snoring, a fatty, warbling sound that sounded like a mix between a wheezing asthmatic and thick purr. I had a little Power kicking around in me, a holdover from the night before, and with a thought and a couple quick words I sent a trickle of it into the little critter, storing it away against a rainy day, so to speak.

I was drained, and in pain. On the ride over I had popped a few more goodies from my box, and I had a full expectation that I would be asleep quick fast and in a hurry. I wanted to be drooling like I had been before all this shit had started up, before I got dragged off the floor to go hunt a dead body.

I got what I wanted, for a little while. Or maybe a long while. With the shed door closed snug and tight, it was impossible to really tell if it was day or night. It didn't feel like a long time, but that could have been the drugs. Horace was still beside me, and a quick check of my pockets showed them empty of bacon. So at least some time had passed.

The debate on whether to turn on the light so I could find and take more pills was front and center on my mind. My head was a little better, but not great, and let's be real—any excuse to pop pills, I took. I was still mighty damn tired, though, so tired I was surprised I woke up at all.

That led me to wondering why I did wake up.

I listened hard, but I didn't hear anything out of sorts. Faintly, through the wall, I was pretty sure I heard Cory watching TV. A few moments more and I realized he was watching something too racy to be on the local channels, and seeing as we didn't have cable out here in the storage sheds, I had to figure he was watching some porno. That was a mental image that would likely haunt me for years to come.

That, or maybe his wife had come for a visit. That wasn't an image I was really looking to have in my aching head.

Faint TV sounds, the faint rumble of some truck driving by on the main road, Horace wheezing. These were the sounds I heard, but they were the usual, normal sounds. Nothing to wake a body up from a sleep as deep as I should have been in.

You deal with enough creepy shit as I do, you learn a couple things, first and foremost being to trust your gut. You start to get a sense for when things are a bit sideways, and I had that feeling now. I had this growing idea that I wasn't alone in my shed anymore. I had that hair-raising, eyes-watching-you sort of feeling. Ever been woken up by someone just staring at you? It was like that.

I lay real still, slowing my breath and trying my damnedest to hear whoever or whatever was in there with me. Horace was making that hard, though, as loud as he snored. I had to get that fucker to lose some weight; maybe then he'd stop snoring. But try as I might, I didn't hear so much as a whisper of cloth rubbing together or someone shifting.

Can you get a CPAP for a possum?

The urge to just close my eyes and let whatever it was out there take me was a real one. Sometimes you're just too tired to muster up much fight, and I could have been having some sort of flashback, perhaps. It's never a good idea to totally rule out the drug angle with me, most people have found.

I could just go back to sleep and act like nothing happened. But then I thought of Kandra's blood-splattered body, and the sight of Morgan, and decided to perhaps err on the side of caution. Moving slowly I reached up, and after a few moments of blind groping I managed to find the long, dangling string of my light and gave it a tug.

The pale yellow light blinded me for a moment, sending a dagger of pain into my eyes. Like an idiot I'd been looking up, right at it, when it came on. You can't go from pitch-black to even my sort of poor lighting without being blinded for a bit, at least, and the likely concussion didn't help matters.

Shielding my eyes I gave the room a quick look over. I didn't see anything out of sorts at first glance. No boogie men, no monsters, no serial killers. More importantly, no cat women with bloody claws. Though, if I was being totally honest, as junky as I kept my place there was definitely room enough to hide at least a fair-sized body in and amongst the detritus mounds of my treasure piles.

I remembered all the work HD and I had put into warding this place up and looked over and up at the back wall of my shed. The skulls were both there, and my stomach sank to see a pale red glow coming from the eyes of the cow skull. There was something happening, something unnatural, past my wards.

Looking inward I saw I was tapped out on Power, so I placed a hand on Horace and began drawing on what I had stored inside him. Turning on the light had woken him, but he was clearly too comfortable in the little blanket nest he'd scrunched up to bother moving. And as drawing Power out of him seemed to do little more to him other than cause him to wiggle a bit so that my hand, which had been resting, was now doing more of a petting motion, he continued to be as unfazed as I was troubled.

I'd tucked away a fair bit of Power in him, more than I could safely hold in myself, actually. I didn't understand how that could work, but then I really didn't know that much about familiars. So I drew a good chunk out, enough to have me fighting ready, I hoped.

Standing up I began to slowly turn in a circle, taking it all in. I couldn't see anything, but there had to be something there. If it had been just me setting things up, I would have figured I set it up wrong, but with HD helping I was certain we'd done it right. So whatever was in here had to be invisible.

I called up a favorite spell of mine, a tiny floating orb that revealed magic and the like. I'd mostly only ever used it to reveal wards, but I hoped maybe it would have other uses.

Sure enough the walls of my shed, up near the top were we'd lined the wards, began to glow.

More importantly I saw a faint shimmer in the corner of the room near the door. As I watched, it became fractionally more stable, a blue-green glow that had the faint outline of a human form. One that I thought I recognized, even through the shifting haze.

It was Kandra.

Uninvited Guest

We stood there watching each other, me all bathed in dingy yellow, her in blue-green. The longer I kept my little orb up, the clearer and more defined she became. She was still whole, the healing the Keening had imparted on her seeming to have stuck with her.

As she became more clear, I was able to see her facial features. Her face was hard looking, but not as angry as it had been. It was a look of determination, not of rage—a look that was locked onto me pretty hardcore. My faint hope that the Keening had managed to send her off to her final reward, and free me from her desire for vengeance, was pretty well and true dashed on the rocks of that look.

It occurred to me that to get the revenge she wanted, I was going to have to lay the smack down on a briar witch who was older, and much more powerful, than me. Someone who knew what they hell they were actually doing. Someone who could turn into a fucking panther, for fuck's sake.

In the epic duel of panther lady versus possum boy I was pretty sure I could spell you out the ending, and it didn't go well for possum boy. My only hope was that Granny had handled it for me. Though if the old biddy had known about this ghost haunting me, I wouldn't put it past the bitch to let it ride as long as possible just to fuck with me.

Kandra wasn't moving, and she also wasn't summoning up thorns and shit to damn near kill me, so I supposed I was ok for the moment. But I did want her gone. If she was just going to lurk around ruining my sleep I was gonna quickly lose my damn mind. And what good would my wards of warning do if I always had something floating around setting them off?

I decided that perhaps I could just get real drunk and that would help me sleep. Again, the concussion plus the liquor was probably a terrible idea, but my life tended to just be a series of terrible ideas and I had survived so far. Granted, I don't know that most folks would agree on my definition of "survival," but I like to set a low bar.

Stepping back to the far wall, I pulled out a beer from a case set on the ground by the mini-fridge. I didn't want to risk some tooth pain from a cold beer to go along with my head pain, so cracking it open, I took a long swallow of warm Steel Reserve. It tasted about as awful as you'd expect, but it was the start of a means to an end. Turning around, I leaned back against the fridge and looked over at Kandra again.

She hadn't moved, not an inch, near as I could tell. It was mighty unnerving, if I was being honest. Ghosts are bad enough, but one standing still as a post and just staring at you? That's somehow worse. I was beginning to wish she'd come whooping and hollering and shaking chains around the room. That would be scary, sure, but not *creepy* scary. It's an important difference.

That's when I got my wish, more's the pity.

Suddenly the spirit wheeled around, facing my shed door. I heard a faint sound, like the dream of an echo, that must have been her howling away so loud that I managed to hear it from the spirit realm. Then she was gone, having rushed through the closed door.

"Uhhh . . ." I managed to get out before every ward in my room began to glow a red so bright it put my bulb to shame.

Then the bulb blew.

Then the wards blew.

Then I panicked and my little orb blew.

And I was back in the dark again.

Uninvited Guest, Redux

I didn't have a clue what I should be doing. My gut said to run, but the only way to run was out the door, which is where Kandra had taken off toward. If she was screaming and running at something, it had to be fucking Morgan. I was not going to run toward a damn panther so it could eat off my face too.

Three times back to back I tried to spill out some words and Power to get a spell of protection out, and each time I failed. I wasn't thinking at all clearly, and my head was pounding so hard I thought it was going to split right in two. Between the fear and the pain I was beginning to think I would never be able to get the spell off. I just wanted my arm protected so I could throw it in her mouth when she tried to eat me! All I could picture was those attack dogs that you see on the news. They always go for the arm. She'd go for the arm too—she had to. That was the rules. Right?

My roll-up door began to rise, slowly at first, then it rattled up so quickly that I thought it was going to skip the track. Going from bright-red light, to pitch black, to light again was doing a number on my eyes. At least it was only moonlight and security light and not the brighter light of the sun. I'd have been blinded forever had that been the case.

That was all secondary, though. What was important was the woman standing there in my door, grinning like a Cheshire cat. A woman whose face tugged faintly at my memory, sending a wave of memories flooding down that I hoped I would get to live to unpack at a later date. Aunt Morgan. Fuck.

She was taller than me, though not by a whole lot, and slim. Her face was lined with a few wrinkles, and her hair was steel gray, but I had a feeling she wasn't all that old. Late fifties, maybe. She had on a dark-blue dress that ran to the middle of her calves and was belted around the waist with one of them belts I always associate with Western fashion—wide, leather, and with silver discs like flowers spaced out across it. Only hers had some carvings on them I suspect you wouldn't find on clothing in your typical Western wear store.

I think she might would have been pretty if not for the fear making me just about wet myself. That, and she had crazy eyes, the kind of eyes that might as well have had a flashing yellow sign that read out "DANGER, KEEP

AWAY." They were deep-brown pools, like a still pond, but when paired with that grin of hers they might as well have been whirlpools of "get fucked."

Still smiling, she stepped inside. Each step she took forward, I took back, leaving as much room as I could manage. I figured I was standing in shadow, basically, so maybe she couldn't see me that well. Though the chance was tiny, it was at least a little bit of an edge. And she wasn't a cat, so maybe she would keep the face eating to a minimum.

"Hello, Howie," she said. Her voice was warm, but I knew better. This woman had killed, and recently. I'd had too many run-ins with nice-sounding things that ended up burning me. See my love life for a host of examples. "It's been awhile."

I kept my mouth shut. I was sitting on G, waiting on O. She was stronger, smarter, all that, but I was gonna go down fighting. Reaching down deep, I started calling up my Power in a big way, sending the veins in my head to pounding which, let me tell you, was less than pleasant, all things considered.

Morgan just laughed. "Men," she giggled, and with a quick flash of her hand like a snake striking and a couple quick words, I went stiff as a board. I was froze solid, locked in place like a tree stump. Beside me Horace was hissing up a storm, curled up in a hunched-back pose, his toothy mouth open wide like a cat. Honestly, it was the most emotion I had ever seen out of the critter.

"Simmer down a bit," she smiled in my direction.

"You too," she said to Horace, reaching out a hand as though to pet him. He was not having it, though, instead curling back and making as if he was gonna bite her. Wisely, she kept her hand clear. I hadn't ever heard of someone getting possum bit, but I had to imagine that it wouldn't feel real good.

She kept her distance, standing a few feet away, her body outlined by moonlight. "Alright, not to be one of those cliché villain types, but we can do this hard or easy. And by that, I mean *on* you, not *for* me. I'm too lazy to drag you to my van, so I would much rather unfreeze you. But I also don't want you trying anything. My problems are with your Granny, not you. Clear?"

I didn't know how I was supposed to respond, not being able to move. But I was in general willing to go along for the ride, I supposed. Not that I could tell her that.

She eyed me for a while then, real hard like. Her face twisted a little bit and she bit her lip, as if she was trying to hold something back. Like she might have lost control for a split second. She was a briar witch, and the older the witch, the madder they got, I'd heard.

"I hope you remember me. We were close once, when you were little. I still remember, at least, and if you do, I think you know I wouldn't hurt you, unless I had to. You're my little Howie Bug."

That was a name I hadn't heard in over twenty years, and if she hadn't been standing in front of me, unlocking those memories, I don't think I'd have been able to place who'd called me that. But she was Aunt Mogga, I remembered. The same time that memory came, my body regained control of itself with a flick of her wrist.

She eyed me warily, but I pretty well instantly tamped down the Power I had been summoning up. I guess she sensed that, because her smiled returned, big as ever. "Howie Bug and Mogga ride again," she cackled.

In a Van Down by the River

I walked along beside her as we left my shed. Horace followed for a bit, hissing all the way, until I managed to shoo him over to the dumpster. "Should I even bother locking up?" I asked her.

She gave a little shrug. "I guess it all depends on how it works out. How much your Granny cares about you."

I laughed, loudly. "Oh, I think you are barking up the wrong tree there," I chuckled, closing my shed and clicking the lock home.

When I looked back at her she had an odd look on her face, but she didn't say anything beyond, "Come on." Together we made our way out past the row of storage units, out to the road. Down a bit, she had parked her van in the lot of a propane company.

The van was a stereotypical mom van, some sort of early 2000s minivan, light-blue in color with some stick figure stickers on the back that showed a woman and three cats. Beneath it was another sticker that read "My kids are purrrfect!"

"Really steering into the whole crazy cat lady vibe, aren't ya?" I asked as I got close enough to read the stickers.

"It's an inside joke, really," she whispered at me with a mock conspiratorial whisper. "I actually only have two cats."

I thought of Kandra's dead body and didn't see the humor. I tried a different tack. "Wasn't real nice of you, blowing up all my wards like that. Spent a good day getting them put in. Waste of fucking work now."

Morgan clicked her key fob and I heard the doors unlock. "You did those? Oof, that's pitiful. Your Granny needs to get you brushing up on your sigil work, because that was just pitiful. Amateur hour in there; I barely had to flex at all to blow right past them. And not a one of any sort of defensive warding. Lazy, just lazy."

"I'll be sure to pass that along next time I see her."

She winked at me with those crazy eyes of hers. "Please do."

Clearly she was unaware of how things had gone down between Granny and me which, as the memories trickled back in, would make sense. Morgan had dipped out around the time my Granddaddy—well, around that time. He had been a much larger part of my life than she had, having given me the bulk of my training. Morgan had spent her time with Granny for the most part.

My guess was she was thinking that Granny took over my training as the heir apparent to the Marsh brand, as it were. She'd no idea that Granny promptly, in effect, told me to fuck off and started honing in on training Krista exclusively. If Morgan wanted to really get Granny's attention, she needed to be kidnapping Krista, not me.

Realizing that, I knew I had to keep the pretense up. At least long enough for Granny to come kill her. I knew she wouldn't be doing it on my behalf, and my going missing wouldn't phase her none or cause her to speed up any. But if I could keep things going long enough, it would keep Krista safe.

I didn't have any desire to die, but I damn sure knew I didn't have any desire to live if it meant I ended up causing Krista to die. On the plus side, me having been at Granny's when Morgan attacked . . . that at least would probably help keep the fiction going, so long as I didn't fuck up too bad.

We climbed into the van, her behind the wheel and me in the passenger seat. The back of her van had all the seats missing, and in place of that were a number of boxes, a pair of chests, and what looked like a little sleeping pallet. It had the look of her living out of there, but she was getting a bath from somewhere, 'cause she didn't stink. Maybe truck stop showers?

The van had a tape deck, and when the car cranked up some sort of hippie music came out the speakers. Nothing I recognized, but Morgan started humming right along as she buckled in. When I made no move to buckle my seat belt she eyed me hard with a pinched, serious look on her face. With a sigh I, too, buckled up.

"So, what brings you back?" I asked. I mean, what the hell else do you ask when a ghost from your past kidnaps you?

Morgan frowned. "Hurricane Irma. It pretty well messed up what I had going on, what living down in the panhandle like I was. So I decided it was as good a time as any to come home and get back what's mine."

"That was a while ago . . . you just been hiding in the county ever since?"

She just smiled a little, real sneaky like. Or what I think *she* thought was sneaky like.

"Right. So what exactly are you here for? What's yours?"

She perked right up then, too damn near Valley girl levels of chipper. "Oh, revenge, mostly. I mean, I'm not really from here, you know, I just kinda grew up near enough that my parents were able to connect me with your grandparents to get me trained right. So it's not like I want to live here, live here. I just kinda . . . want to be able to visit when I want. That, and kill your Grandmother. Let's be honest, that's the main reason."

I opened my mouth, then closed it. Morgan seemed content to hum along to the music and not make small talk, so I let her keep on with that. And I had to deal with the mother of all conflictions. I mean, I didn't exactly pray for Granny's death, but I certainly wasn't opposed to it. But again, I had to keep Krista safe.

But on the other hand, Granny being dead would probably put Krista in a better place. Me too. But . . . much as I hated the old bitch, she did keep the peace in Jubal County. There were a number of players at hand—all stronger than me, mind you—that held no special love for me. I mean, I wasn't on their bad list, but I was certainly fucked with less on account of the fear of Granny.

And, well, let's be honest, I was probably on a lot of their bad lists. The King and Preach came to mind . . .

My talk with HD also came to mind. I had a plan to get out from under the old bitch's thumb, and after all, she had to die sometime. She was old as hell. If I could just buy some time, I could come out on top maybe. You know, if the drugs didn't kill me first.

And, well, Granny also, more than anyone, kept my Daddy in check. Which might have been the most important thing of all—at least for me, in the short term.

So while Morgan killing Granny might be a good thing, it might also be a bad thing. It was something I had to chew on. Did I help Morgan? Help Granny? Do nothing?

Knowing me, I would try and do nothing. I mean, that was really my usual state of being, if folks would just leave me the fuck alone. But since it looked like all I had was time at the moment, I decided that I could chew on it a bit. Worry that bone.

Though the real worry that was starting to hit was the fact that I had walked out without my box of drugs. And if I went too long without that . . .

I glanced over at the crazy cat hippie lady beside me and wondered if catnip could get you high. Maybe she would at least have some green on her, maybe even some shrooms or the like. Never could tell with hippies. I would hold off on asking for a bit, though. I wanted to see where we was headed first.

She drove the van through Elk Grove and hit the county roads with a clear destination in mind, it seemed to me. If she'd been up this way since Irma, she'd had plenty of time to refamiliarize herself with the roads and such. And my guess was she'd been spying on us, which was probably how she found me.

Jubal County was especially pretty at night. Moon shining bright like it was, you could see the outline of things, but the darkness sorta glossed over all the imperfections. The woods looked like something out of a fantasy movie, and the fields shone with a pale blue almost.

We slowed once, Morgan hitting the brakes as a pair of does went scampering across the road, and then a moment later came a faun. It still had its spots, and its legs were still a little ungainly. I was just glad I'd had my seatbelt on or I'd have smacked my head, most likely. Not that I'd dare admit it to Morgan. She was probably, maybe, the enemy after all. Definitely a killer, even if she wasn't turning her claws on me just yet.

Our general direction took us toward the Camp, which I had guessed would be where we were headed. We would be headed to her witch house, 'cause why else would she have killed Kandra? I mean, she could have just been some sort of weird serial killer, but I had my doubts. I wondered how we was gonna get there though without going through the Camp, however.

Instead of turning off onto the road that I'd been down so recently, she kept driving past the Camp cutoff. A couple miles down was a bridge, and it was there that she pulled off, the wheels finding a faint rut. I'd never noticed them before, because stuff like that was common. Folks liked to fish around bridges, so little trails that led under them weren't all that noticeable.

The van bounced and its shocks groaned on the uneven roadway. The ruts led under the bridge, where there was just enough room for the van to pass along the edge of the creek. There was barely a half dozen feet to spare, which, for a driver that was frequently fucked out of his gourd, was entirely too narrow for a driveway. I'd have ended up parking every car I ever borrowed in that creek.

Morgan slowed, easing the nose of the van near a stump that jutted up on the creek bank. Out beyond it I could see that the ground was far too muddy to drive on, and I saw that there was going to be a hefty walk in our future. It was all ankle-deep patches of water set between mud holes and knotty cypress trees. My skin already started to itch with the bug bites I knew were forthcoming.

But as the van nudged up beside that stump, a sigil flared briefly to life on its bark, a deep-purple set of lines that looked like a drunken attempt to sketch a monkey. At the same time a matching glyph came to life on the hood of the vehicle, and what had been in front of me no longer was. It'd had been mostly illusion, and as I watched the shallow ruts carried on, veering away from the creek and deeper into the swamp.

I tried not to look impressed.

Judging from Morgan's face, I'd failed.

She laughed.

Run Through the Jungle

We did have to walk a bit, but not as far as I had been dreading. It did eventually get too muddy for a minivan to tackle, but it turned it from a walk of miles to a walk of about five hundred yards. I still got ate the fuck up with bug bites, though. Either bug bites didn't bother Morgan or she had some of HD's luck, 'cause I didn't see her slap once.

I love a swamp, and a swamp at night is a special sort of magic. Not all the bugs were bad. Little flashes of light dotted the area as fireflies made themselves known and danced their little dances. And the frog song was in full force, a steady thrumming noise that drove some folks nuts but that I had always found soothing. Coupled with the moonlight bleeding through the treetops to send a silver blanket down on the land below, well, fuck me if it wasn't gorgeous.

We'd gotten a good ways away from the creek, but I could hear it gurgling faintly in the distance. But what caught my ear the most was the faint tinkle of wind chimes. These were not the *thunks* of Granny's bamboo chimes—these were a more delicate metal sound. The sound of "keep away, active witch workshop" for those who knew the warning signs.

Ahead of us, in the direction of the chimes, the undergrowth grew steadily thicker. Thick brambles seemed to block our path, but as Morgan approached the brush parted before her with a wave of her hand. I had to walk quickly in her wake to keep from getting snagged as they fairly quickly returned to their original state as she passed.

"Briars never hurt their own," she said as she walked, the first words she'd spoken since we'd left the van.

I could see a small hut just up ahead and knew it would be her witch house. It was a small thing, maybe fifteen feet by fifteen feet, set up against a thick willow tree. The low-hanging bows arched over and around the walls, partially hiding it from view. They grew all around, covering everything but a door and a small stained glass window. Hanging from them I could see the wind chimes, small rusted things that waved in the night breeze.

Above the door was a pair of small skulls—I think of rats—each painted a blue so dark that they looked more black in the gloom. On them were painted a thorned spiral, and as we neared their eyes glowed teal. Morgan ignored them so I did the same, instead watching her hands as they flicked back and forth in a few motions, paired with low words.

Lightbulbs, which were tied to limbs with small lengths of twine, began to glow with a clean bluish light, bathing the little clearing amongst the briars with soothing light. Within the hut itself a yellow light came to life, sending a square of gold out to shine into the night.

"How'd you do that?" I asked. I didn't see any wards or the like, and this was a new spell to me for sure. "Those didn't sound like any words I've heard before."

Morgan laughed. "Your Granny does love her secrets, doesn't she? The reason the words I use are different are because your family uses Shelta for their words, and I . . . don't. The words don't actually matter, not really. Same with the all the hand waving and other mumbo jumbo. All that is to just help focus your mind. That's what really does the magic."

"Oh, right," I said, as though what she said made a lot of sense. I'd be unpacking that for a while, I reckoned.

"So, welcome to Manyath," Morgan said softly, waving a hand around her in a slow circle. Stepping over, she opened the door. Through the narrow crack I could see shelves thick with all manner of jars and the like. But I only got a tiny glimpse, as my eyes fell on the two cats that came threading out through the gap.

One was immensely fat, stark white with no markings. Its head, which had to be normal sized, looked tiny on its rotund body. The other, which wasn't skinny by any stretch of the imagination, was also fairly white, though it had a few patches of orange. It was quiet, but the fat one began to squawk, a weird yell of a meow that came out as more of a "MRAH!"

"Hey, babies," Morgan cooed, rubbing them both around the ears as they rubbed against her legs, as though trying to trip her. "This is Cream," she said, patting the fat white cat, "and this little puddin' is Peaches."

They were no Horace, but they seemed nice enough, I supposed. When Morgan stopped petting them, the fat one came over to me and meow-yelled at me, and I obliged it by giving it some scritches as well. The other one kept its distance.

There were a couple of folding lawn chairs which, judging from how new they looked, had been bought with my kidnapping in mind. Morgan settled into one and was promptly buried in a thirty-pound white cat that she held like a baby. The other curled up around her feet, watching me.

"So, what now?" I asked, taking a seat across from her.

"Now, we wait. I figure your granny will be along in a day or two to rescue you. And if you behave while me and her fight, I'll let you live." She put her forehead against Cream's and nuzzled him. She then began talking to the cat in a sort of baby voice. "Yes I will, yes I will, if he's a good lil' puddin' like you!"

With a grunt she lifted the cat up and set it back on the ground, where it proceeded to croak out its odd meow. She ignored it, however, shifting her focus back to me. "I mean, it's the least you can do, seeing as you managed to muff up my little ambush. I'd been planning that for weeks, you know."

"Next time give me a little notice, and I'll arrange to be elsewhere," I snarked.

"No, really, you hurt me a bit." She shifted in her seat and pulled her dress up. It rose far higher than I had ever anticipated seeing on the woman till it was up near her hip and I could see a small corner of the waistband of her undies. But sure enough, there were a few red welts there that could have been the pattern of a shotgun blast. Only they weren't holes, they looked more like . . . zits, or bug bites. Other than that, though, it was a damn fine leg, I had to admit.

"Well to be fair, I didn't know it was you, exactly. I thought you was a panther."

Morgan, still holding her dress up, winked at me. "Really more of a cougar."

That pretty well tied my tongue. I ain't got much going for me but a quick tongue, but getting hit on by a woman who helped raise you a bit—well, that has a way of getting a body out of sorts. And it was pretty on-brand for Alabama, sadly. I think I did manage to mutter a hyperintelligent, "Um . . ."

"Anyone ever tell you how much you look like your grandfather?" she asked, lowering her dress back down, her brown eyes boring into me.

"Maybe?" I squeaked.

She grinned like . . . well, a cougar.

It was shaping up to be a long kidnapping.

Marsh, Interrupted

Sometime around midnight I managed to get the point across that I had a girlfriend, and one that I was happy with. I ain't never been all that big on monogamy—one of my endless failings, according to a host of my more recent exes. But Anna, like Lidda once had, warranted my best efforts.

Morgan had fully shucked the dress by the time I got the point across, and so needless to say she went to bed in a bit of a huff. And by "went to bed," that, I learned, meant she took the hut while I got frozen in place in a chair. I didn't know if that was gonna be an every night thing, or just the nights I pissed her off, but come the morning I was ready to do whatever it took to not have to spend the night like that again.

My body was stiff in ways it had never been stiff before, a whole body muscle ache that I hoped to never experience again. Morgan was back to her chipper self, strutting out the witch house with a smile on her face and a couple of tins of cat food for her kitties. Once they were fed she'd untuck me, and I'd spent the next half hour working out kinks while she "fixed" breakfast. I suppose I got my love of Pop-Tarts from her, because when she got back from the van she had a half dozen varieties for me to choose from.

I had a bad itch running down my spine. The kind of itch that could only be scratched by the contents of my box of oblivion. Carefully, I set about broaching the subject with her in the most politic way I could muster.

"I need drugs. Pretty bad."

She looked up from the book she had settled in to read, Peaches laid across her lap like a bearskin rug. "I know. I could feel them in your magic."

"So . . ."

She shook her head. "Consider this a chance to get clean. When your Granny is gone, I want you around with your head clear. She might have let you get away with that, but I won't."

I laughed a little, but it wasn't something cutesy. I could hear the hard edge to my laugh, and I could see that she did as well. "That ain't an option. I'll sit here and play nice, but only if you get me what I need."

She rose to her full height, glaring down at me. "You don't tell me what to do. There's a new sheriff in town, and you are going to start acting right, so help me God."

I stepped to her. She was taller, but my eyes met hers. "I think if you ask around, you'll find that I'm pure hell on sheriffs. And I don't take kindly to murderers."

That's when things got kinda nasty.

I don't think she really wanted to fuck me anymore a couple hours later when she finally locked me down again in frozen mode. It's pretty bad when you can out-crazy the crazy, I reckon.

I'm a Fun Guy

The good thing about being frozen is that it stops the need for drugs. The bad part is when you unfreeze half a day later, it all just comes rushing back, and twice as bad. You don't need to see all the details—we ain't got time for all that. Suffice it to say there were some tears, some wails, a pretty apt impersonation of the Keening, a whole lot of cursing, and a shouting match that made what happened before she froze me look like a playground squabble. She was lucky I wasn't a fighter, or we might have scrapped.

What matters is I wore her down, she went into her hut, and when she came back out she had a few treats.

Nothing she had would scratch the itch, not exactly. Only the meth would do that, and it was pretty clear she wasn't about that life. But the handful of shrooms she had, if they were what I thought they were, would at least distract me enough that I would be tolerable. For a few hours, maybe.

A seed of a thought hit me. I grabbed all but a couple of the mushrooms and went to pop them into my mouth. Pausing, I looked at her. "Gonna join me?"

She frowned. "I only use these on special occasions."

"And I know you ain't trying to poison me how, exactly?"

If I'd learned nothing else about Morgan, it was the fact that her mood could change on a dime. So when she smiled big and popped them in her mouth, I wasn't terribly surprised. "Ok, fine," she said, grinning through a mouthful of dried mushrooms. "Getting a touch of the spirit world in me for a bit will get my mind right to take out your Granny."

I followed suit. They were gritty and tasted pretty terrible, actually. But soon enough I knew they would get our brains altered just right so that we'd be high as kites, if only for a little while. High, but even better, in that weird state that made the spirit world and us more in touch. In touch enough that stuff that normally couldn't act on us could.

God, I hoped Kandra was around and that she would briar up Morgan like she'd done me.

We were sitting there in the chairs waiting for things to take hold, so to make conversation, I asked what I really wanted to know. "Why'd you kill her?"

"Who?"

"Kandra. The punk woman you clawed up not far from here. Shitty thing to do, to someone who meant you no harm."

Morgan sighed. "You trying to harsh my mellow, Howie? Not very cool of you. But I had to. What if she'd seen my place and gone back and told people? And then those people came and explored? You know how it is here in Jubal County—everything gets back to your Granny. If she knew that my witch house was back occupied, then she'd have known I was back, and I'd have lost the element of surprise. I couldn't risk that."

I shook my head sadly. "That's some bullshit logic to me. Lots of other things you could have done. A simple illusion—anything would have been better than killing."

She looked hard at me. "If anything, you should be the one feeling bad. It's because of you that the poor thing's life was wasted."

How do you even respond to something like that? I just kept my mouth shut, closed my eyes, and waited for the high to kick in.

PLANS GONE AWRY

"You're haunted . . . it's her, isn't it?" Morgan said about ten minutes later.

I opened my eyes and the world had that faint sheen of the other world about it. I could see the outline of Kandra growing stronger in my sight, not far from where Morgan sat. My "aunt" looked puzzled.

"Why didn't you just break it? Why would you keep a haunting?" Her lip curled as her eyes ran up and down my body, lingering on the fraying bandages on my wrists. "This one looks nasty. Did it hurt you?"

She was so focused on me, she didn't even see the vines sprouting up from the ground.

Puddles of purple-red darkness blossomed beneath the back chair legs, and from them came vines covered with crimson-tipped thorns. They shot up in a flash and within moments had begun to ensnare Morgan, wrapping around her like a quick-moving python. As I watched, dark red thorns buried themselves into the briar witch's flesh.

With a shout I rose to my feet, summoning up every ounce of Power I still had in me and feeding it into my right arm. I leapt over at the struggling woman as she squirmed within her chair, fighting against the bindings. One crow-hop later I sent my fist flying into her face with enough force that I felt at least one bone in my hand snap like peanut brittle.

Morgan went flying back. Her skin shuddered and pulsed red-blue. Clearly I had triggered some wards which had likely saved her life, but they did nothing to stop the momentum of the blow. Her skin ripped in two dozen places as the thorns tore at her flesh as she broke free of the vines.

Her back hit the witch house and she went through it with another pulse of light, this one a red-gold that was weaker than the first. I heard the shattering of dozens of glass jars. Some I was sure were just spell materials, but some I was just as sure were spirits.

Through the Morgan-sized hole in the wall I saw pulses of light and saw her climb to her feet. I was about to turn and run when . . . something . . . tackled her to the ground. I heard a scream, and a roar, and the sounds of fighting.

And then I could feel magic, lots of magic—lots more magic than I had ever been able to summon up—all flying around inside that hut.

Magic like that, I could fight something like the King and have an actual chance of winning. But how? How did she manage—

The far wall of the hut cracked wide, from the sounds of things, and something with a few too many limbs went hurtling out. I figured now was as good a time as any to run, but suddenly Morgan came leaping through the door, her face enraged. She was clawed up something fierce, and her hands were themselves turning into things sharp and pointy and rife with the ability to perforate my hide.

Something long and snakelike shot out of the doorway and wrapped around her waist, and with a scream she was ripped back inside. I heard more crashing, and glass shattering, and the air began to look like the northern lights.

Magical energy and formerly contained things were filling the air. The air was shimmering in a rainbow of colors, as though the hut had turned into a giant prism. Tiny things were flitting around, sprites and fairies from my best guess. I was almost certain I saw a redcap go running off into the underbrush, which pissed me off because I knew someone would need to handle that before it found the Camp and caused more trouble.

That's when the hut exploded, the force of which sent me flying back. One the plus side, I didn't hit my head, wrists, or ankle. On the down side it's because I landed in a giant briar patch, one so thick I could barely see anything happening outside of it beyond flashes of light and the sounds of screams.

Fuck me.

The Devil Makes Three

I had quickly learned that thrashing about was just a recipe for those thorns to dig in deeper. Slow and steady was the only way to free myself, but with all the drama happening just a bit away it was kinda hard to keep that sort of focus. Every sound of some critter roaring or Morgan flinging some spell caused me to flinch, which caused the briars to score my flesh, which caused me to flinch more. It was a bloody cycle.

Caught up in that bullshit like I was, it took me a few moments to realize I wasn't alone in those brambles. It was only the flicker of some motion to my right with some color to it, that clued me in. Eyes wide, I turned my head and locked gazes with that fucking redcap.

It was maybe two feet tall, with one of them old-style knit hats like a medieval peasant would wear. Like a . . . lazy beanie? Hell, I don't know how to describe it. But the most important detail was it was dyed a dark crimson which, from everything I'd ever heard, came from the creepy fucks dipping those hats in the blood of whoever they killed.

I was lucky that this one seemed to be missing any sort of weapon. But as it started to crack a wicked smile my way I could see that it had more than enough fuck-off-big teeth to handle my tangled ass. The whole thing looked like it hadn't hardly ever eaten a meal; the thing was rail thin, but its fingers, which ended in some gnarly blood-red nails, looked that like they had some wiry strength to them too.

It started creeping up on me, muttering lunacy under its breath, no doubt working the small magic that made the briars leave it untouched and unhindered. Normally a redcap isn't a huge problem—it's only with numbers that they get tricky—but I was tapped out on magic and all caught up.

The real pisser is my granddaddy taught me that a crucifix would usually send most of them running. But my spiteful ass had refused to wear one since about middle school, having decided that a stance of "to hell with churches" was the ultimate act of rebellion in religion-loving Jubal County.

Somewhere in my junk pile of a shed was a perfectly good wooden cross on a necklace he'd given me for my fifth birthday. Carved it himself. Just like this redcap was about to carve me up.

That left one option, and I was damn certain I would fuck it up. Looking the little bastard right in the eyes, I started trying to recite every Bible verse I could remember. "Jesus wept. Turn the other cheek. Yeah, even though I walk through the valley of the shadow of death, I won't fear any evil."

Verses could have the same effect, I'd been told, but this may come as a shock to you: I wasn't exactly a star pupil in Sunday school. Instead of turning in fear, or whatever it was supposed to do, the damn thing just sorta cocked its head at me for a moment, then started back heading my way, getting almost close enough to jump. I started trying to get myself stood up so I could make at least some attempt at fighting, shouting all the while. "Jesus wept! Goddamn it, Jesus wept! God loved the world and sent a son or something! Valley of death!"

All of a sudden the thing started, looking back in the direction of the witch hut. It snarled a bit, then poof—it fucking vanished. All that was left behind was one of its teeth, which had fallen to the ground as it disappeared. I heard it go running off through the briars, running away from whatever was headed in my direction. I looked and saw that Morgan seemed to have gotten things under control, and she was looking in my direction.

Fuck.

I had almost managed to extricate myself from the briars when Morgan came stalking over to me. She was looking like a hot mess, I had to say. She was cut up and bleeding all over the damn place and even had a pinky missing, it looked like. If she felt it, she didn't act like it, though, which was maybe the scariest thing of all.

"You managed to fuck up everything."

"Welcome to my life," I said, resigned to my fate.

"It took me years to gather up that stuff, years to gather enough goodies to level the playing field between your granny and me for even *one* fight. And now that's shot to shit." All that was said really calmly, which is why I flinched real hard when she started to shriek at the top of her lungs and stomp her feet.

A minute later the shrieking stopped as suddenly as it began. "I should kill you," she said matter-of-factly.

"Well, if I have a say in the matter, I'd really rather you didn't. Things being equal and all."

She stared at me. For a long time. A long, long time. Several minutes. I was too scared to move or say anything in case it convinced her to settle on killing me. Finally, she turned and started walking back into the clearing.

The hut was just a pile of rubble, the chairs blown into the bushes. When I finally spotted her cats, I was surprised to find them unharmed and up the willow tree. I wouldn't have thought Cream's fat ass could climb. That, at least, made me happy.

She was surveying the wreckage, shaking her head.

"You live. Because in the end, I brought this on myself, didn't I? Killing that woman—in the end, it caused all this. Fucking karma." She spat. "Your granny always said it was the little details you ignored that would haunt you the most. God, I hate when that bitch is right. And I don't intend to worsen my karma by killing you. At least not yet. Not till I put her under."

"If it helps at all, she wouldn't have come for me," I offered. "Not long after you left, she stopped any learning I was getting. She ain't too fond of me."

She looked at me for a second. "Makes sense."

What did that mean, I wondered?

"Get out of here. I'm going to gather up what I can save and leave too. I need to rethink a few things." She turned to me, then grinned. This time it wasn't a nice grin. "But don't worry, I'll still be around somewhere. And I'm going to keep my eye on you."

I turned and started out of the little clearing, intending to get while I still could, when Morgan called out one last thing. "I took care of your little haunting for you, by the by. Maybe in the future you will handle your business, yeah?"

I nodded mutely, then started off at a quick jog.

THE CAVALRY

I was halfway back to the Camp when I met HD and Krista coming through the swamp. To say I was surprised was a gross understatement. My uncle had his shotgun in hand, and Krista was so brimming with magic that even in my weakened state I could feel it coming off of her.

As soon as I came into sight Krista ran to me, hugging me as tight as she ever had. It hurt, what with all my briar scrapes, but I didn't care. "You came for me?" I asked, almost shocked beyond words.

Krista was crying and nodding her head. I looked over at HD.

He shrugged. "My gut said something bad had happened, and I just kept feeling like I needed to come to Morgan's witch house. Didn't take a genius to figure that one out."

Him, I expected. Krista, though . . .

"I can't believe you came," I said, pulling her back into a hug.

After a moment she took a step back and wiped at her eyes. "I can't hide forever, I guess." She looked down at her feet. "And it's not fair for you to have to carry the load all the time. Maybe . . . maybe I could start to help you out sometimes."

"Where's Morgan?" HD asked, his mind clearly on task even if his niece and nephew had gotten sidetracked.

"Leaving. I sorta fucked things up for her, so she's gonna dip for a bit. I'll tell y'all all about it on the way back to my shed."

I glanced behind me in the direction of where the hut had been. All I could see was peaceful swampland. I turned back and, throwing an arm around Krista, we started back for civilization. The feeling of being watched was pretty strong on me, but then what did that matter? Morgan? Granny? Something else? I had folks who had my back, and I wasn't too shabby myself in a pinch. We'd be ok.

"So you know how you said you wanted to help?" I asked, fingering the tooth of the redcap. I was going to have to handle that sooner rather than later, but I knew what to do there, at least. "What do you know about spell jars?"

THE BACK MATTER!

About the Author

Born and raised in South Alabama, Bob is an author, podcaster, tabletop game designer, and all around hot mess. His cause of death will most likely result from one of the hitchhikers with he picks up reckless abandon. A study in contrasts, he once skinny-dipped at a wedding and is also an Eagle Scout. He has two useless college degrees, has roadied for bands, and broke his wrist in a wall of death at a Divine Heresy show. He's written for video games, designed board games, and owns a disturbing number of roleplaying games. When he was eight he give a camel a coke in Israel and got flashed in Paris. When he grew up he watched a monkey steal a man's wallet in Costa Rica. He's made passible podcasts, filmed terrible short horror movies, and been the producer on a trio of albums you've never heard of. Thriving on the groans of those he has punned around he spends far too much time nervously laughing. He once dug up a dead cow in a creek thinking it was a human cadaver and has a cousin that's a water witch. In college he gave haunted ghost tours (even though he's pretty sure ghosts aren't real). He's been stalked, gave a Prophet a lift, and been stagger drunk in more states than he would care to admit.

Growing up, he was always jealous of the wide variety of jobs his favorite authors listed in their 'about the author' sections, not fully realizing what a hellscape he was lusting after. So to that end Bob has been in no particular order: a warehouse clerk, a roadie for a band, pizza delivery guy, grocery store bag boy, telephone survey giver, inventory manager, quit Walmart after only three days, and currently works in IT. Learn from him sweet children, and flee now to the woods and leave behind the world of men.

More relevant he wrote this book, some other books, and has been published by a number of other folks with questionable judgement. The fictional things he writes sometimes come weirdly true. He lives in the middle of Alabama with his amazing LadyWife, the Kiddo, and a number of increasingly portly cats.

You can learn more at **www.talesbybob.com**

Reviews!

Did you leave a review? In the immortal words of Mathew McConaughey: "It'd be a lot cooler if you did."

Email List!

If you want to keep up with news about my books, this is the best way! I'll never sell or share my email list, and I promise to never bother you more than once a month (unless, like, its super-mega-secret important). To sign up go to my website: **www.talesbybob.com**

Patreon!

If you want even more Bob content, then go check out his Patreon. It's full of short stories, flash fictions, even draft copies of books. Big news also gets announced there before anywhere else, along with sneak peaks of book covers and other behind the scenes content. A popular series on there are 'The Marsh Dispatches' which is an ongoing series of essays written from the perspective of Howard Marsh the Methgician. Check out **www.patreo n.com/talesbybob**

Transparency!

When I started out, I had no other authors that I knew well enough to ask questions about sales numbers, social media growth, etc. I had no idea if my sales numbers were good, bad, or somewhere in-between. But seeing as I'm a big believer in the concept of '*be the change you want to see*' I started sharing all that information in hopes that it would motivate other authors to do the same. And even if they don't, at least this information is available to anyone who wants to know what those types of stats look like for a small time author like myself. So if you visit my website you can see all sorts of behind the scenes information each month, like how my social media grew (or shrank), how sales were, what I tried differently that month, etc. I also break down my stats around my book launches and get into the nitty gritty of each major in person event I do. Check out **www.talesbybob.com/transparency-project**

Education!

I have been helped by countless other creatives and authors along my journey. So anything I can do to pay that help forward, I do. That's why as much as possible I try to keep a host of free resources on my website folks to learn from. If I get paid to teach a workshop, I usually turn it into a youtube video and share the powerpoint I used along with it. If I get asked the same question enough times I will turn it into a blog post or video. I also offer up 'intern' opportunities for folks who want to learn in person sales. And if you want something more in depth, check out my book "Create Your Way to Freedom! How

To Be A Big Success From Someone Who Isn't!" Check out **www.talesbybob.com/education**

Podcasts!

Bob does a lot podcasting. You should go to his website, **www.talesbybob.com** (noticing a theme here?), and check them out. Most of them are related to books in some way, but not all! His best known historically has been Books, Beards, Booze.

Book Clubs!

Want to read this book as part of your book club? Reach out! If you are close enough, I might come speak to it (especially if yall have good snacks). If you are farther away, I might be available to speak to your group remotely. At the bare minimum I will shoot you an email with some bonus content of some sort, and some book club discussion questions. Just us the contact form on my website, **www.talesbybob.com/contact**

About Bearded Bard Inkworks

A real human book publisher, who puts out novels and ttrpgs!

Here at Bearded Bard Inkworks, we are human people, who put out books, and things like books. Booky things. With actual pages. And ink. Except when they're digital of course. Either way, we're absolutely people, and not at all three octopuses pretending to be book publishers. Just look at the top hats. Only a human could be so fashionable.

Look, we love books here at Bearded Bard Inkworks. We do. But we also love rpgs. And general weirdness. So we seek out authors who are exploring unique spaces, while also generating cool tabletop games. Because who doesn't love the idea of finding that next book they love, and then getting to play a game in that world?

Learn more at **www.beardedbardinkworks.com**

Struggling with Drug Addiction?

If you or someone you know is struggling with drug addiction and want to get help, then call the number below. It is the Substance Abuse and Mental Health Services Administration help line, a confidential, free, 24-hour-a-day, 365-day-a-year, information service, in English and Spanish, for individuals and family members facing mental and/or substance use disorders. This service provides referrals to local treatment facilities, support groups, and community-based organizations. Callers can also order free publications and other information.

1-800-662-HELP (4357)

For more information you can visit their website here:

www.samhsa.gov/